* * * * * * *

"Nick, I - - - I need your help."

I could tell by the sound of her voice that there was something very wrong. It was also clear to me that whatever it was it had to be something really serious for her to even consider calling me, let alone actually picking up the phone and talking to me. In the years since our divorce had become final, she had not called me once.

"What's the matter?" I asked.

"Jeff has disappeared," she blurted out almost hysterically. "He left on a trip to Hartford, Connecticut, but he never arrived."

"I'm sure there's a reasonable explanation," I said in an effort to smooth her ragged nerves and to get her to calm down.

"I'm telling you he never arrived. He was going to a conference on computer games or something, but he never arrived."

"Are you sure?"

"Damn it, Nick, he never got there," she yelled.

"Calm down. Maybe, he checked into a different hotel,"

* * * * * * *

Other titles by J.E. Terrall

Western Short Stories
- The Old West
- The Frontier
- Untamed Land
- Tales from the Territory

Western Novels
- Conflict in Elkhorn Valley
- Lazy A Ranch (A Modern Western)
- The Story of Joshua Higgins

Romance Novels
- Balboa Rendezvous
- Sing for Me
- Return to Me
- Forever Yours

Mystery/Suspense/Thriller
- I Can See Clearly
- The Return Home
- The Inheritance

Nick McCord Mysteries
- Vol – 1 Murder at Gill's Point
- Vol – 2 Death of a Flower
- Vol – 3 A Dead Man's Treasure
- Vol – 4 Blackjack, A Game to Die For
- Vol – 5 Death on the Lakes
- Vol – 6 Secrets Can Get You Killed

Peter Blackstone Mysteries
- Murder in the Foothills
- Murder on the Crystal Blue
- Murder of My Love

Frank Tidsdale Mysteries
- Death by Design
- Death by Assassination

BLACKJACK, A GAME TO DIE FOR

A Nick McCord Mystery

by

J.E. Terrall

ISBN: 978-0-9916232-7-3

This is a work of fiction. Names, characters, and incidents are either a product of the author's imagination or are used fictitiously, and any resemblance to actual persons, living or dead, is purely coincidental.

Printed in the United States of America
First & Second Printing / 2009 – www.lulu.com
Third Printing / 2015 – www.createspace.com

Cover: Front cover designed by Phyllis Terrall
Photographed by J.E. Terrall

Book Layout/
Formatting: J.E. Terrall
Custer, South Dakota

BLACKJACK, A GAME TO DIE FOR

A Nick McCord Mystery

To Cathy

CHAPTER ONE

The sun was setting over the wooded hills across Lake Mendota. It cast a warm glow on the tranquil blue green waters. The thin clouds that drifted high overhead filled the sky with colors of reds, yellows and oranges as the sun slowly sank lower and lower in the western sky. A gentle breeze blew in off the lake making the air feel fresh and cool. Yet, not so cool as to make us want to go inside and miss the beauty of the sunset.

I was sitting on the porch swing with the most beautiful woman in the world. As we slowly rocked back and forth, I began to think of her and what we had together. She was leaning up against my side with her long blond hair gently brushing against my cheek and her long shapely legs tucked under her. The gentle breeze lightly pushed her soft hair away from her beautiful face, and her exciting cobalt blue eyes sparkled as she turned and looked at me. I couldn't help but wonder what it was that she could see in me, an ex-cop.

"What are you thinking about?" Monica asked.

"You," I replied as I leaned closer to her and kissed her lightly on the lips.

For the moment it was nice to just sit on the porch swing and listen to the birds singing in the trees as we watched the colors of the sky slowly change. The sky grew darker and darker with each passing moment, but we didn't care as long as we were together.

As time slowly passed by, I began to think of what was ahead for us. We had been living together in Monica's town house on the outskirts of Madison, Wisconsin, ever since our return from Arizona. I have to admit that I had not even given my apartment in Milwaukee a second thought. Maybe it was because it was much smaller than Monica's town house, or maybe it was because I was content to just stay here with her. Either way I was happy right where I was now.

Monica and I were currently without jobs. Since we still had some money left over from our Arizona venture. We were not in critical need of finding jobs at the moment. In fact, we had decided to take a couple of weeks to just be together and enjoy each other's company before we faced the cold cruel world of job hunting.

I guess I couldn't help myself, but my thoughts turned to questions like, how was I going to provide for this wonderful woman sitting beside me? I was sure that she would not have a problem getting a job at a university somewhere. After all, she had been a history professor at the University of Wisconsin, and she was well known and respected in her field.

However, my prospects were a little more uncertain. I was nothing more than a cop. I'd always been a cop. In fact, I had even been a Military Policeman while I was in the Army. I really didn't know much else. There was little chance that I would get a very good recommendation from Captain Sinclair of the Milwaukee Police Department. I had left the Department without giving him any kind of notice, and that never sets very well. Plus, he had been rather upset with me for leaving the way I did.

Although I had little or nothing to offer Monica at the moment, being with her just seemed to feel right. I felt that it was getting about time for us to make some sort of decisions as to what we were going to do. Decisions that could determine our future together.

Just as I turned my head to look at Monica and ask her what she thought we should do, the phone rang inside her town house. I didn't really want this time with Monica to be interrupted, but I had always found it difficult to leave a ringing phone unanswered.

From the look on Monica's face, I got the impression that she didn't want our time together disturbed any more than I did. Somehow I got the feeling that she was wondering what the future would hold for us, too.

"I'll get it," I said as I reluctantly lifted my arm from behind her and stood up.

After walking through the balcony doors into the dining room, I turned and looked back outside as I reached for the phone. Monica was still sitting on the porch swing, but she was watching me as I picked up the receiver.

"Hello?"

"Nick, this is Sharon."

"Sharon?"

"Sharon Holcome. You know, your ex-wife?" she said rather sarcastically.

"Yes, I know who you are. You just caught me by surprise. I never expected you to call me here. In fact, after our last conversation I never expected to hear from you again."

"Where else was I going to get hold of you? You're never in Milwaukee anymore."

"I didn't think I had to check in with you anymore," I said rather harshly, not liking the tone of her voice.

"I don't care where you spend your time," she said sharply.

This conversation had already gone further then I had wanted. I had no desire to get into a verbal fight with her. I had had enough of that when we were married. I certainly didn't need it now.

"Is there some reason for this phone call, or are you going to make me guess?" I asked in an effort to get right to the point.

There was a long period of silence before she responded. I thought I could hear her taking a deep breath before she continued as if she was trying to get her thoughts together, or possibly get her feelings under control. It wasn't hard to notice the change in her voice when she came back on the phone.

"Nick, I - - - I need your help."

I could tell by the sound of her voice that there was something very wrong. It was also clear to me that whatever it was it had to be something really serious for her to even consider calling me, let alone actually picking up the phone and talking to me. In the years since our divorce had become final, she had not called me once.

"What's the matter?" I asked.

"Jeff has disappeared," she blurted out almost hysterically. "He left on a trip to Hartford, Connecticut, but he never arrived at the hotel."

"I'm sure there's a reasonable explanation," I said in an effort to smooth her ragged nerves and to get her to calm down.

"I'm telling you he never arrived. He was going to a conference on computer games or something, but he never arrived."

"Are you sure?"

"Damn it, Nick, he never got there," she yelled.

"Calm down. Maybe, he checked into a different hotel," I offered as a possible explanation.

"He wouldn't do that without letting me know," she insisted.

"Maybe his company changed his reservations. Have you checked with his company to see if they might have had some change of plans?"

"Yes. That was the first thing I did. His secretary told me the name of the hotel he was planning on staying at. I called them, but he isn't listed as having checked in."

"Let's start at the beginning and take it one step at a time," I suggested. "Do you know for a fact that he actually got on the plane to Hartford?"

"Yes, of course," she replied sounding rather upset with me for having the gall to even ask. "I took him to the airport and saw him board the plane myself."

"Okay. Where was he flying to, I mean what city?"

"His destination was Hartford, Hartford, Connecticut. He was flying into the Springfield-Hartford Airport."

"Was he planning on going anywhere else before the conference that you know of?"

"He said that he had to make a quick stop in Groton, Groton, Connecticut, before going to the conference in Hartford."

"Do you know why he was going to Groton?"

"He was to deliver something to a company that makes submarines for the Navy, or something to do with them."

Do you know the name of the company?"

"No. When I called his hotel in Hartford, they told me that he had not checked in yet."

"Do you know how he was getting from the airport to Groton?"

"He was to pick up a car at the airport, then drive to Groton to make a delivery of some kind of computer software thing, I think. I don't know anything about computers and things like that. After he made the delivery in Groton, he was going to return to Hartford for the conference," the tone of her voice was calmer, but still showed her frustration.

"Did he rent the car at the airport or did his company provide one?"

"He rented a car at the company's expense. And, yes. I've already called the car rental company. They said he picked up the car as scheduled."

"So then we know he got to Connecticut. Do you know if he was planning on returning the car when he got back to Hartford?"

"No. He didn't intend to return the car until the conference was over. He told me that he might like to have it in case he decided to go somewhere else. He was planning on returning the car to the airport when he was ready to fly home. What difference does that make?" she asked.

"If he rented a car, we can have the police see if they can find it for us."

"I never thought of that," she conceded.

"You said that he might like to have the car in case he decided to go somewhere. Do you have any idea where he might have been thinking about going?"

"No, he didn't say. He mentioned that when he was not busy at the convention, he might do a little sightseeing in the area. That's all he said."

"Do you know if he made the delivery in Groton?"

"I don't know," she yelled into the phone. "Damn it, Nick, are you going to help me or just ask a lot of stupid questions."

I could tell by the sound of her voice that she was near panic and that my questions were just upsetting her more. It was clear that I would have to meet with her if I were going to get the kind of cooperation I needed. I would need to find out where Jeff had gone, what his timetable was, and then track him step by step until I found him.

I glanced over at Monica. She had come to the door and was listening to at least my side of the conversation. It must have been clear to her that there was something wrong. She looked a little worried. I felt that I needed to give her some idea of what was going on.

"Hold on just a moment, Sharon," I said into the phone.

Without waiting for an answer, I put my hand over the mouthpiece of the phone before talking to Monica.

"This is my ex-wife. Her husband has disappeared. She's asking me for help in finding him."

"Is this unusual or does she often call you for help when she has a problem?" Monica asked.

"It's very unusual. She wouldn't call me unless she had no other recourse. She sounds really desperate."

"I think we should try to help her," Monica said.

I looked into Monica's eyes in an effort to see if she really meant what she said. I was sure that she did. I was also sure that she had some reservations about it, but then so did I. It was impossible for me to tell if Monica's reservations were because it was my ex-wife, or because she didn't like what she had heard while I was on the phone.

"Are you sure?" I asked.

"Yes," she replied.

While still looking at Monica, I took my hand off the phone and put it to my ear.

"Sharon, where are you calling from?"

"I'm calling from home."

Her voice sounded like she had regained some control of her emotions. She answered my questions clearly and without raising her voice.

"You still live at the same place in Chicago?"

"Yes."

"Okay. We'll be there in the morning. We'll need to get as much information about Jeff's travel plans as possible. I want to know as much detail as you can find out or remember. The more I know, the more I can help. Do you understand?"

"Yes. I'll write down everything I can remember," she agreed.

"Okay. I'll see you tomorrow morning."

"Nick, will Doctor Barnhart be coming with you?" she asked.

I noticed that the tone of her voice had changed slightly. I could remember hearing that tone in her voice when we were married. If she didn't want me to do something simply because she didn't happen to like it, she would say it with the same kind of a whiny tone in her voice she was using now. It didn't set well with me, but this was not the time to get into a discussion of petty jealousies. If I could help her, I would; but it would have to be on my terms or not at all. I was not about to put up with her trying to control my life again. I'd had enough of that when we were married. After all, our life together was over and had been for several years.

"Yes. She will be coming with me. Is that a problem for you?" I asked in a slightly harsher tone than I had intended.

"No. It's okay. I'll see you in the morning," she replied, her voice suddenly changing to a more acceptable tone.

As I hung up, I looked over at Monica. It had been clear by the sound of Sharon's voice that she did not want me to bring Monica to her house. I had made it equally clear from the tone of my voice that I would not help her if Monica were not allowed to come with me.

"She doesn't want me to come with you, does she?"

"No, she doesn't. But she doesn't have anything to say in the matter."

"Are you sure that's a good idea?" Monica asked.

"No, but that's the way it's going to be. You either come with me, or I don't go. It's that simple. I'm not going running off to who knows where without you."

It was clear by the look on Monica's face that she understood me to mean actually what I said. I reached out and put my arm around Monica's shoulder, gently turned her around and walked with her back out onto the balcony. We returned to the swing where I sat close to her and put my arm around behind her.

It was a long time before either of us said anything. We sat watching the stars slowly fill the darkening sky. Although I was concerned about Monica's feelings, I couldn't help thinking about what could have happened to Jeff.

I didn't know very much about Jeff. In fact, all I knew was that he was some kind of computer whiz and that he made software games for computers. I didn't even know for sure the name of the company he worked for. I had met him only once. As I recall, he seemed like a rather nice fellow. A little quiet and reserved, maybe, but nice enough.

"Nick?"

"Yeah?"

"I was thinking," Monica said, then paused as if to gather her thoughts. "What would you think if we started our own business?"

"That sounds like it might be a good idea. What kind of business did you have in mind?"

"I was thinking that we could start a business as private investigators," she said as she turned her head and looked at me.

I looked at her for a moment without comment. It was as if she knew what I was thinking. I had not said anything, but I had thought about that very thing once or twice over the past couple of days. The fact that our trip to Arizona had been paid for by a man looking for answers to what had happened to his brother helped make the idea seem like a good one. The fact that we were not licensed private investigators did not lessen the value of the idea. That was something that I was sure could be easily remedied.

"What kind of investigations would you suggest we do?" I asked, although I was pretty sure that I already knew her answer.

"I wouldn't want to hide in the bushes and take pictures of unfaithful spouses or anything like that. That seems so - - dirty. I was thinking more along the lines of looking for missing people or something along that line. What do you think?"

"Something like what we are going to do for Sharon?" I asked as I looked at her.

"Yes. Just like that."

"I'm a pretty good investigator, and you certainly have a very useful background," I said thoughtfully. "I think it's a good idea. We would make a good team. Where would you want to set up an office?"

"Do we really need an office? Couldn't we work out of, say, here?"

"I don't see why not," I said after taking a moment to think about it.

"We could get an office if you think we need one, or we could get a different place, say, in Chicago or Milwaukee if you think that would be better."

"No. We could work out of here. We could set up the spare bedroom as sort of an office. It would be more of a place to keep records, do research and make phone calls. We wouldn't have to meet with clients here. In fact, I would prefer not to meet with them here," I said.

"We could meet with clients, say, in their home, or in a restaurant, or some other public place," I said as much to hear myself think as to express my thoughts to Monica.

"That sounds good."

"We could also take jobs for companies that need someone or something found, or to investigate internal crimes, such as Industrial Espionage, embezzlement or theft," I said as I thought about the kinds of cases we might want to handle.

"We could do that, too."

"How would you suggest we start?" I asked.

"We could put a website on the Internet and get an e-mail address and a post office box as a way for people to find us and get in touch with us," she suggested, the sound of excitement growing in her voice.

"That would be a good idea. That way we wouldn't have to have a fancy office. A good computer, a good fax machine, a private phone line for the business and we could be in business."

"We would need a very good website," she added. I know a guy in the computer department at the university who could help us set up a website."

"Great idea."

Monica squeezed my hand and smiled at me. I was sure that she was looking forward to working together as much as I was. I could think of nothing that I would rather do for the rest of my life, than to spend it with her. Working side by side would give us more time to spend together.

"I think that would probably work pretty well. We can get started setting it up as soon as we find Jeff," she suggested.

The idea of starting a new business with Monica at my side had caused me to forget about Sharon and her problem, at least for the moment. Maybe that was because I really didn't want to think about the possibility of having to go to Connecticut. I was more interested in Monica's ideas of us working together.

"Speaking of that, I think we should get some sleep. It's about a two and a half-hour drive to Sharon's place. I would like to get an early start," I suggested.

"Okay," Monica replied with a smile.

I took my arm from behind Monica, stood up and reached out to her. She took my hand and we walked back into the town house. We went into the bedroom and got ready for bed. As I laid down on the bed, Monica curled up beside me. The feel of her naked body against me was comforting. She had a way of making me feel as if I was the most important man in the world.

"Nick?"

"Yeah?"

"Do you love me?"

I turned and looked into those cobalt blue eyes of hers. My first thought was that she was worried about meeting my ex-wife. I'm not sure how other women feel about such things, but Monica seemed to be concerned about it.

"Yes, I love you very much," I said as I leaned close to her and kissed her.

Monica returned my kiss with the same deep passion that I had shown her. I wanted her to know that she had nothing to worry about from Sharon or anyone else. She was the only woman for me.

It wasn't long before she wrapped her arms around my neck and rolled up over me. She rose up and looked down at me.

"Make love to me," she whispered in her soft sexy voice.

Now that was one request that didn't have to be made twice. I reached up and gently pulled her face down closer to mine. As our lips met, I let my hands slowly slide down over the smooth skin of her back and up over her firm butt. The feel of her firm breasts pressing against my chest, and the feel of her warm naked body stretching out over me, and the feel of her lips pressed against mine sent my desire for her to new heights. As we kissed, our passion for each other soared.

It wasn't long before I rolled her over on her back. I leaned down over her and kissed her. As our passion for each other grew, I lowered myself over her. In no time at all we were making love to each other. Our desire and need for each other was filled with passion. I don't know what time it was when we finally drifted off to sleep, but I slept well with her still in my arms.

CHAPTER TWO

Morning came a little too early to suit me. I woke well before the alarm was set to go off. Even with our lovemaking before we went to sleep, I found myself waking up thinking about the call from Sharon and the panic in her voice.

After lying in the bed looking up at the ceiling for what seemed like hours, I carefully rolled out of bed in the hope of not disturbing Monica. I went over to the window and pulled the curtain back a little, then sat down on the windowsill.

While looking out at the lights reflecting off the smooth surface of the lake, I tried to think of what might have happened to Jeff. Had he really just up and disappeared, or had he simply changed his plans. At this point in time there was no way to know.

Jeff seemed to be a nice enough guy, although he seemed a little shy and reserved. I had to wonder if there was something going on at home that Sharon had failed to mention. After having spent several years with her, I knew that she was not the easiest person to live with. Giving it some thought, I doubted that there was any serious problem at home because Sharon seemed too upset for that. She would not have called me if they had a fight or something along those lines. I was also well aware of the fact that Jeff wouldn't be the first guy to leave his wife by simply disappearing and not returning home.

The more I thought about Jeff and his sudden disappearance, the more I realized that I didn't really know him all that well. The one thing that I was going to have to do was to find out just what it was that made Jeff tick. I needed to know what it was that motivated him, and what he actually did for a living. In addition to all that, I needed to find out what the name of the company he worked for was and what he did besides make computer games. It also wouldn't hurt if I had some idea of what his hobbies were, if he had any.

"Nick, are you all right?"

I looked over toward the bed. Even in the darkness of the room I could see Monica sitting up and looking at me. In the dim glow from the outside light, I could see that she was worried. I could also hear it in her voice.

"I'm fine, honey. Go back to sleep. We don't need to get up for another hour or so."

"Since we're both awake, why don't I get up and fix some breakfast. We can talk a little before we leave," she suggested.

That didn't sound like all that bad an idea. It might help if we talked about Jeff, even if she didn't know him. We might even come up with an idea or two that would help us understand why he didn't show up where he was supposed to be.

"Okay, but I think I'll take a quick shower," I said.

I got up from the windowsill and went into the bathroom. As I stood in the shower and let the warm water run over me, I thought about what we were going to do. I had to admit to myself that I had a bad feeling about this whole thing. I knew that it could be something as simple as Jeff checking into a different hotel, or it could be something far more serious. The trouble I had was that I didn't know which, and I didn't have anything solid to help me lean one way or the other.

Once I finished showering and had gotten dressed, I went out to the kitchen. Monica had fixed bacon, eggs and toast for breakfast. The table was set and she was waiting for me.

“Nick, would you prefer that I stay here,” she asked as I sat down at the table.

I looked at her. Her question had caught me by surprise. Her eyes often told me more about what was going on in her mind than anything else. I could see in her eyes that she didn’t really want to stay here and wait for me to return.

“No. I want you to come with me.”

“Are you sure?”

“Yes. I’m sure. We’re partners, remember?

“Yes,” she replied softly.

“Would you rather wait here?” I asked.

“No.”

“Than that settles it. We go together.”

With that said and out of the way, I began eating. Nothing more was said about it while we had breakfast.

After Monica finished her breakfast, she left the kitchen and went into the bedroom. I could hear her moving around in the room while I sat at the table drinking a second cup of coffee.

It occurred to me while I was drinking my coffee that I had already gotten used to being around her. The thought that we would be going into business together gave me a pleasant feeling. Working with her would keep her near me, and I liked that idea.

I had just finished my coffee when Monica returned to the kitchen. She was wearing a pair of nice fitting slacks and a blouse that showed off her gorgeous figure. Her long blond hair laid gently on her shoulders, and her cobalt blue eyes sparkled in the morning light.

“Is this okay,” she asked as she stood still and let me look at her.

“You look very nice, very nice indeed,” I said with a smile.

“Thank you,” she said obviously pleased with my response.

"I was thinking. Maybe we should pack a few things. There's a very good chance that we could be going on to Connecticut."

"How long do you think we might be gone?"

"I don't know, but I think we should pack for, say, at least four days. If we are gone any longer, we can go to a Laundromat and wash some clothes, or buy a few things."

"Okay," she agreed.

I stood up and walked over to her. I took her hand and led her back into the bedroom. We packed our bags without much conversation. It seemed that we were both lost for the moment in our own thoughts.

As soon as we were finished packing and had cleaned up the kitchen, we carried our bags down to her little sports car. After putting our bags in the trunk, we started for Chicago. We hadn't been on the road for very long when Monica looked over at me.

"I'm sorry," she said.

"Sorry about what?" I asked as I glanced over at her.

"For being jealous."

"Jealous of what?"

"You and Sharon."

"I can assure you that you have nothing to be jealous about. There is nothing left between Sharon and me. It was over years ago."

"I love you," she said as she reached over and put her hand on my leg.

"I love you, too," I replied.

We didn't have much to say to each other after that, but that was okay. We loved each other and that was all that mattered. The miles passed by rather quickly. Being close together seemed to be enough for now.

It was shortly after nine in the morning when we pulled up in front of Sharon and Jeff's house. It was a rather nice looking tri-level house in an upper middle class neighborhood. The house was in excellent repair and the yard was well groomed. It looked like the kind of a house that most of America would want to live in.

"We're here," I said as I switched off the key.

Monica just looked at the house while I got out of the car and walked around to open the door for her. She took my hand as I helped her out of the car. As we walked toward the house, the front door opened and Sharon stepped out on the porch.

"That's your ex-wife?" Monica asked, seeming somewhat surprised.

"Yes."

"She is a good looking woman."

"Yes, but not the nicest person in the world to live with," I replied softly as we walked toward the front porch.

"I expected you to be here earlier. I've been waiting for you for hours," Sharon said sharply, her anger showing in her voice.

I stopped and glanced over at Monica as if to say, "See what I mean", but I refrained from saying anything that would cause more friction in an already tense situation. Sharon's sharp tongue and the fact that she completely ignored Monica angered me, but it was also clear that Sharon was anxious and worried. I could understand that. Even so, I didn't feel that there was any reason for her to take it out on us. After all, we had dropped everything to come to her aid. It was uncalled for and I wasn't going to put up with it.

The thought came to mind that I didn't need this. I was about ready to turn around and let her try to find Jeff on her own. I think I would have done just that if I hadn't already told her that I would do what I could to find Jeff.

"Let's get something straight, right here and right now. If you want us to help you find your husband, then you better start acting like a human being. We can turn around and go back to Wisconsin just as easy as we can go on to Connecticut. In fact, it would be a lot easier for us to return to Madison. So, do you want our help or not?" I asked rather sharply.

Sharon seemed surprised at the frankness of my comments. I got the impression that she thought that I would do anything she wanted regardless of how she treated us. It apparently had not occurred to her that I would leave her to solve her own problems in a heartbeat, if she continued to be nasty about it.

As I waited for Sharon to decide if she wanted our help, I could feel Monica squeeze my hand. Just the way Monica held onto me let me know that she was feeling a little uncomfortable. It was also clear that Monica understood Sharon's anger and could as least sympathize with her.

I watched Sharon as she looked at Monica, then back at me.

"Yes, I want your help," Sharon conceded quietly.

"Then let's go inside. I have to have some information even it you think it's not important.

Sharon turned and walked into the house. Monica and I followed her into the living room and she motioned for us to sit down on the sofa. Monica sat down and I sat beside her. Sharon sat in a large chair on the other side of the coffee table.

"Can I get you anything?" she asked.

I noticed that she didn't look at Monica when she asked. It was obvious that she felt if she ignored Monica, she might not exist, at least in her mind.

"No. You just have to answer some questions, then we will be out of here," I said, not wanting to be here any longer than necessary.

"Okay," she replied softly.

The tone of her voice had changed some. I got the impression that she might be ready to cooperate and help me find Jeff. She was making every effort to remain calm. She was hurting and I had not made our visit any easier for her.

But by the same token, she had not made it easy for Monica, either.

"Who does Jeff work for?"

"He works for Games Unlimited here in Chicago."

"Just what does he do?"

"He works in the games division. He makes and tests computer software games. Some of the games are very complicated," she replied.

From her reply it was easy to see that she was very proud of what Jeff did. I guess she was justified in that as anyone who knows very much about computers tends to impress me.

"Does his company do any kind of government work that you know of?"

"I guess they do, but Jeff doesn't work in that part of the company. He just works on software for games."

"Are you sure?"

"Well, I think so. Yes. He's always talking about this game or that game he's working on. I don't really understand much about them."

"Jeff told you he was going to Groton. Did he tell you where he was going in Groton and what he was delivering there?"

"No, not really. He said that his company asked him to hand deliver a piece of software to a company in Groton."

"Did he tell you the name of the company?"

"He might have, but I don't think so. I think he just said that the company makes submarines for the Navy."

"It shouldn't be very hard to find out the name of the company. Did he give you any idea what the software was for?"

"No. I don't think he knew what it was for himself. All he told me about it was that he was just delivering it."

"Okay."

It was becoming clear to me that Sharon didn't know very much about Jeff's work or his activities. What I needed to know now was what his plans were. Where he was going and what he planned to do there.

"Do you have a copy of Jeff's itinerary?"

"Yes. I'll get it," Sharon replied as she got up.

I watched her as she left the room. As soon as she was gone, I turned and looked at Monica.

"What do you think?" Monica asked.

"I don't know, but I think we need to make a stop at Games Unlimited and talk to them. If this "piece of software", as she puts it, was for some government project, especially having to do with submarines, I doubt they will tell us much. But on the other hand we might get lucky. If they know one of their employees is missing, they might help us find him."

Monica was about to say something when she looked toward the door. I turned my head and looked toward the door in time to see Sharon coming back into the room with a sheet of paper in her hand.

"This is Jeff's schedule. It includes his flight numbers, times of departure and arrival, where and when he was to pick up a car, and where he was to stay. Everything I could think of. It even has the date and time of a speech he is to give at the conference."

I took the sheet of paper and quickly scanned it to see if I had any questions. It appeared that Sharon had done a pretty good job preparing it. She had even included the telephone number of the hotel where Jeff was supposed to be staying. I couldn't think of any additional questions to ask her at the moment.

"Sharon, is there any chance at all that he had to change hotels for some reason?"

"I suppose there could be, but not that I know of," she replied. "His secretary said that he was scheduled to stay at the hotel listed in his itinerary."

"By the way, does Jeff have any hobbies?"

"No, not really. He spends a lot of his free time on his computer. I guess you could say that computers are his hobby."

"We're going to check this all out. We'll be in touch with you as soon as we hear anything. Are you planning on going anywhere?"

"No. I want to be here in case he should call," she said.

"I take it he still has not called you?"

"No," she replied sadly. "I called the hotel again, but they said that he had not checked in, yet. I was told that some of the others that were there for the conference had already checked in."

"In that case, we'll get started," I said as I stood up. "We'll call if we have any news at all."

I reached out for Monica's hand as she stood up. I took her hand and led her to the door. Sharon followed us as far as the front door.

As we started down the sidewalk toward Monica's car, Sharon called out to me.

"Nick?"

I stopped and turned around to see what she wanted.

"Be careful," she said.

I was a little surprised at her concern for me, but I nodded that I would, then turned back around. With Monica's hand in mine, we walked to her car.

"Where to now?" Monica asked as she got in the car.

"Our first stop is Games Unlimited."

As I walked around to the other side of the car, I glanced back toward the house. Sharon was standing on the porch watching us. The look on her face was that of a woman who was confused and maybe a little lost as to what to do next. I guess I couldn't blame her much for that. I know that I would be lost if anything happened to Monica.

I got in the car, started it and then pulled away from the curb. I had a pretty good idea where Games Unlimited was located. It was in one of those fancy, high-tech industrial park type places south of the downtown Chicago area just off Interstate 57.

"If my memory serves me right, General Dynamics has a place in Groton, Connecticut, that makes submarines," Monica said casually.

I glanced over at her and asked, "How do you know that?"

"My uncle was career Navy. He was stationed on a submarine that was based out of Groton. I remember him saying something to my father about General Dynamics making submarines in Groton."

I glanced over at Monica again as I turned onto the Interstate. This beautiful woman beside me never ceased to amaze me.

Monica's little sports car cruised along the Interstate. It wasn't long before we arrived at the industrial park where Games Unlimited was located. It was easy to spot the building with its name in big bold letters across the front of the two-story building made of concrete and glass.

It was a fairly modern building, probably not more then three or four years old. The grounds were well groomed with trees nicely spaced around the parking lot in front of the building. The one thing that caused me to wonder if we would be able to get in to talk to someone was the tall wrought iron fence that surrounded the property. As I got closer to the drive into the parking lot, I could see the gatehouse manned by security guards.

"I don't know if we're going to get to talk to anyone that could help us," I said as I looked at the security surrounding the building.

"Maybe if we ask to talk to Jeff, we might at least get to talk to his secretary," Monica suggested.

"Good idea. It certainly won't hurt to try," I said as I turned in at the gate.

As I pulled up and stopped in front of the gate, a rather large security guard with a gun on his hip stepped out of the guard shack. He looked over the little sports car and smiled.

"May I help you?" he asked as he leaned down and looked inside the car.

"I would like to talk to Jeff Holcome, please."

"Your name, please?"

"Nick McCord."

"Just a moment," he replied then stepped just inside the guard shack and made a call.

I watched him as he talked on the phone. He was good at keeping his facial expressions unreadable. He did look at us for a moment while he listened to whoever it was on the other end of the line. I still couldn't tell what was going to happen when I saw him hang up the phone. He stepped up to the car again and bent down.

"Mr. Holcome's secretary will meet you in the front lobby. Please park in the visitors' parking area just to the left of the main entrance to the building."

"Thank you," I replied.

I waited until he stepped back in the guard shack and hit the button that opened the large steel gate. As soon as it was opened, I drove through and followed the signs to the visitors' parking area. I parked the car and got out. After helping Monica out, we walked toward the main entrance of the building.

As we approached the security guard just inside the front doors, I noticed a woman in her mid-to-late thirties inside the building. She was just standing there watching us, or more like waiting for us. I got the feeling from the look on her face that she was worried about something.

"May I help you?" the guard said as he stepped in front of us.

"Yes. We're here to see Jeff Holcome's secretary."

"She's waiting for you. You will need a visitor's pass. Would you sign in here, please," the guard said as he pointed to a book on a stand.

I stepped over to the book and wrote my name and the time in the book. I then handed the pen to Monica.

As I waited for Monica to sign in, the guard gave me a visitor's badge to clip on my shirt. While Monica clipped her badge on, I looked through the heavy glass wall at the woman. She seemed to be growing very impatient to see us.

"You are allowed only in the office area," the guard instructed as he opened the door.

"Thank you," I said as I stepped back and let Monica go in ahead of me.

"Excuse me, are you Mr. McCord?" the woman asked, the tone of her voice showing a hint of apprehension.

"Yes, and this is Monica Barnhart."

"I'm so glad you came. I'm Janet Marshall, Mr. Holcome's secretary."

"It's nice to meet you. We have a few questions that I would like ask," I said.

"Not here. In my office, please. There are too many eyes and ears here in the hall."

She immediately turned and started down a long hallway. I looked at Monica as we followed her. I was sure that I could see the same surprised look on her face that I must have had on mine.

The hallway was almost void of people. However, a quick look around did reveal several security cameras keeping watch over the halls. I could see no reason for Janet to be so nervous. Greeting visitors had to be pretty routine for her. There had to be some other reason for her nervousness, but I couldn't think of what it might be.

Janet turned and entered an office. On the door were the words 'Jeff Holcome, Director of Games'. It struck me as kind of a silly title, but I was sure that it was appropriate.

"Mrs. Holcome said that you would most likely be stopping by to talk to me. She seems quite worried about Jeff, I mean, Mr. Holcome."

"Tell me, Mrs. Marshall - - -."

"Miss."

"Sorry, Miss Marshall. Tell me, is this an accurate outline of Jeff's itinerary?" I asked as I reached in my pocket and took out the paper that Sharon had given me.

Janet looked at the paper, then up at me. I thought I could see from the expression on her face that there might have been something left off, or there was something there that shouldn't have been. I wasn't sure which.

"Well?" I asked.

"Miss Marshall, all we are interested in is finding Jeff. We are not interested in what he might be doing or why he is doing it," Monica said softly.

Miss Marshall looked at Monica. The expression on her face changed slightly indicating that she might be able to relate to Monica better than to me.

"I don't know if I should say anything, but Mr. Holcome seemed very worried about this trip."

"What makes you say that?" I asked.

"He seemed rather nervous and that was not like him. He always seemed to look forward to these conferences, and seemed to enjoy them. It gave him the chance to spend time with other computer people like himself, something he really didn't get to do much around here."

"Why would he be nervous this time?"

"I don't think he liked the idea that he had to deliver some software to the Navy."

"But I thought it was to go to General Dynamics," I said hoping to find out if that was where the software was to go.

"It is, but it still goes to the Navy. General Dynamics makes submarines for the Navy."

"Do you know why he didn't like the idea?" I asked.

"He didn't say, but I think he was concerned about taking something that might be, you know, secret."

"Was it secret?"

"I don't know. Jeff, Mr. Holcome, didn't say."

"Didn't say or wouldn't say?"

She thought for a moment before she replied.

"I'm really not sure."

"What do you people do here?"

"What do you mean?"

"Do you produce software for things other than games?" Monica asked.

"I'm not supposed to talk about that. I'm not even supposed to know about that. I wouldn't know if I hadn't overheard Mr. Wilcox tell Jeff not to let the disk out of his sight and get it delivered as soon as he got to Connecticut," she said nervously.

"What else did you hear?" I asked.

"Nothing," she replied quickly, almost too quickly.

"You came up with the idea that it was dangerous for Jeff just because you overheard someone tell him not to let a disk out of his sight?" Monica asked, the expression on her face indicating that she found that hard to believe.

"Yes, but you have to understand something. Mr. Wilcox is head of a special department. No one really knows what they do there, but rumor has it that they do work for the Military from time to time. No one outside that department is allowed in their area of the building."

I took a moment to look at Monica. She was looking back at me. This was getting to be more interesting by the minute. If what Jeff had taken to Connecticut was something for the Navy, this whole thing could get rather sticky, to say the least.

I had a feeling that Miss Marshall didn't really know anything that was going to help us find Jeff. Yet, I had this feeling that she was keeping something from us. It was time to move on, but I didn't want to leave without knowing everything about Jeff's movements and his job.

"Is there anything else you can tell us, anything at all that might help us find Jeff?" I asked.

"What do you mean?"

"Do you know of any other plans that Jeff might have had that were not on his itinerary?"

Miss Marshall looked at me, then at Monica. Her hesitance to answer my question made me sure that she knew something but was afraid to tell us.

"Please, Miss Marshall, tell us whatever it is you know. It may help us find Jeff," I said.

"I don't know if I should tell you. He didn't want anyone to know."

"To know what, Miss Marshall?" Monica asked.

"He said he would have a couple of days when he didn't have anything scheduled at the conference. He told me that he might go over to the Knollwoods Resort and Casino and try his hand at a little cards."

"Does he play a lot of cards?" Monica asked.

"No, I don't think so. But he has been working on a game that includes different card games like Poker and Blackjack. He told me one afternoon when we had lunch together here in the office that he had worked out a system for Blackjack. He was hoping to get a chance to try it out and see if it works."

"So he was planning to try his new system out at Knollwoods Resort and Casino. Is that right?" I asked.

"Yes."

"What kind of system?" I asked.

"He didn't tell me. He just said he was going to test it. I don't think he wanted his wife to know he was going to do a little gambling. I don't think she approves of gambling."

"I'm sure she wouldn't. I want to thank you for all your help," I said.

"You will let me know when you find him, won't you?"

Miss Marshall's voice showed her deep concern for Jeff.

"Yes, of course," Monica reassured her with a smile.

I took Monica by the hand and we left the office. As we walked down the hall toward the main entrance, I couldn't help but think that there was more to this than meets the eye.

"Where to now?" Monica asked as we walked past the guard.

"We go home," I said as I quickly squeezed her hand.

Monica is one very smart woman. She took the hint and said nothing more.

As we walked to the car, I walked very close to her. She didn't seem to mind, but I was sure that she wondered just what we were going to do next.

"I think it's time to follow Jeff's steps, one at a time," I said once we were outside and away from the guard.

"Why did you say we were going home?"

"Because I didn't want that guard reporting anything else."

"That's what I thought."

"Did you see the way he was watching us? He was listening to every word we said. I also think we should not talk about our plans in your car, either."

"You think that they may have bugged my car while we were inside?" she asked as she looked at me.

"I don't know, but I don't want to take any chances. They certainly had the opportunity while we were visiting with Miss Marshall."

We got in the car and immediately drove off the grounds.

CHAPTER THREE

As we drove past the guard shack and left the grounds of Games Unlimited, I noticed that the security guard stared at us as we left. It seemed to me that he watched us with a little more interest than I thought was necessary, but then it was his job to keep an eye on those coming and going. I turned Monica's sports car out onto the street and headed north toward the entrance ramp to the Interstate that would take us back toward the downtown Chicago area.

Checking in the rearview mirror, I observed a black sedan as it pulled away from the curb. I had noticed that it had been parked a few hundred feet down the street from the entrance to Games Unlimited when we drove out, but I didn't remember it being there when we went in.

At first I didn't think much of it, but when the car stayed well back, changed lanes every time I changed lanes and stayed exactly the same distance behind us all the time, I began to wonder about it. It didn't take me long to realize that whoever was in the car was following us. The fact that the car had been parked outside the gate caused me some concern. I could not be sure if those following us were from Games Unlimited, or if they might be some other interested party in what we were doing and in where we were going. At the moment, I couldn't think of anyone else that might be interested in what we were doing, so I was inclined to think that it was probably Games Unlimited.

"Are you hungry?" I asked as I glanced over at Monica.

Monica turned her head and looked toward me. I nodded my head slightly to indicate that her response should be 'yes'. She took the clue and responded.

"Yes, I am a little," she said rather casually.

"How about picking up a couple of cheeseburgers and malts and finding a nice park somewhere to eat. It's a beautiful day for a picnic."

"Sure. That sounds like a great idea."

I drove off the Interstate at the next ramp and watched as the black sedan followed us. When I reached the top of the ramp I turned left and the sedan followed right behind us.

"This looks good. How about we get something here?" I asked as I pointed at a drive-in restaurant.

"That would be fine," Monica agreed.

The black sedan was still behind us when I pulled into the drive-thru lane of a Dairy Queen restaurant. I ordered cheeseburgers and malts for both of us. After getting them at the window, I pulled back out onto the street. Within a block we had the sedan behind us again.

We drove to a small park only a few blocks away. I parked the car in the small parking area off the street and shut off the engine. I found it interesting that the black sedan continued on past the entrance to the park without so much as slowing down.

As I watched the car disappear around a corner, I turned around and began to look for the pick up car. That is the car that would tail us after the first one was gone. It was a common practice when tailing someone.

As soon as the black car was out of sight, we got out of the car and walked over to a picnic table where we sat down to eat our lunch. Being as subtle as I could, I looked around while I unwrapped my cheeseburger. It was then that I noticed another sedan of the same make and model as the car that had been tailing us earlier, but this one was a light blue. It had pulled up to the curb and stopped on the other side of the park, but no one got out of it.

I avoided looking directly at it. Instead, I sort of watched it out of the corner of my eye. No one got out of the car, which didn't surprise me. I could see that there were two men in the car, and one looked as if he might be talking on a phone or two-way radio. I couldn't be absolutely sure which from where I sat. The only thing I was sure of was that they were watching us. I was feeling just a little paranoid, but I tended to do that when I'm convinced that I'm being followed or watched too closely.

"I think that black car was following us," Monica said, then took a bite of her cheeseburger.

"I think so, too. Don't look now, but there's another one on the other side of the park, behind you and a little to your left."

"What are we going to do?"

"I haven't decided yet, but I'll think of something. We had a black sedan follow us from Games Unlimited. Now we have a light blue car on our tail. It may be hard to lose both of them. They seemed to be very good at trailing someone."

"I don't think they are very good. We've known they were following us from almost as soon as we left Games Unlimited."

"True, but they still may not be easy to lose."

"What happens if we don't lose them?" Monica asked.

I took a bite of my sandwich and looked over at the car as I gave her question some thought. I was trying to decide if it made any difference if we were followed or not. At this point in time, I didn't see that it really mattered very much.

"Probably nothing. If they're determined to follow us, I guess they will be following us to Connecticut," I said with a grin.

"Do you think that's wise?"

"My guess is that they would like to know what happened to Jeff as much as we would, maybe more. If they lost Jeff, then there's a good chance that they've lost their disk as well. If I had to guess, these guys following us are more interested in finding the disk than they are in finding Jeff. In either case, one should lead us to the other."

"So what's next?"

"We finish our lunch and then we go to the airport. We'll try to fly out of Chicago on the same flight that Jeff took. I want to follow in his tracks as close as we can."

"Okay, but do we know when he flew out?"

"Yes. It's on his itinerary with time and flight number. We'll fly out this afternoon, if we can get tickets."

Monica nodded her head in agreement. I wasn't all that crazy about being followed, but on the other hand they might prove helpful if things got a little messy later on. Besides, I figured that we might lose them when we boarded the plane. If not, I was sure that I could lose them at the other end if we changed our minds and decided that it was in our best interest to ditch them.

After we finished our lunch, we headed toward O'Hare International Airport. The light blue car followed us until we turned into the long-term parking lot. I noticed that the light blue car did not follow us into the parking lot, but went on by toward the terminal.

After parking Monica's car, we grabbed a shuttle to the terminal. When we arrived at the terminal, we went directly to the United Airlines ticket counter. We bought two one-way tickets to the Hartford-Springfield Airport. We also checked our bags to our destination.

We had a little time on our hands so we decided to pay a visit to one of the bars located on the concourse to wait until it was time for us to board the plane. After ordering drinks, we sat down at a table in the corner where we could see who was there. From our position in the room, we could also see everyone who came in or went out. I was hoping to get a look at who was following us.

"What do we do now?" Monica asked.

"We wait."

"For what?"

"For whoever is following us."

Monica looked at me, then picked up her glass and leaned back. She didn't drink from it. Instead, she just looked at it and sort of played with the straw in the glass. I was sure that she was wondering what we had gotten ourselves into, and I couldn't blame her for that. I was having the same thoughts. I was just hoping that we didn't get ourselves in over our heads.

It wasn't long before a man dressed in a dark suit came into the bar. He stopped at the door and looked around the room. The man tried to make it look as if he was looking for someone else in the bar, but I knew he was looking for us.

He then went up to the bar and sat down. I watched him over the rim of my glass. It was easy to see why he had sat down where he had. From there he could keep an eye on us in the mirror behind the bar.

"There's our man," I said softly. "The one who just sat down at the bar."

"How do you know?"

"He's watching us in the mirror. My guess is that his partner is at the ticket counter finding out where we're going and probably buying tickets."

It wasn't long before a second man showed up. He sat down next to the man at the bar. They talked like they were old friends, but I could see that they were watching us more than they were talking.

I took time to get a good look at the two men. I wanted to be able to recognize them if I were to see them again, even in a crowd.

I had just finished my drink when the announcement for our flight came over the address system.

"That's us. You ready?" I asked.

As I stood up and reached out a hand to Monica, I noticed that the two men got up and left the bar ahead of us. I smiled as I slipped my hand behind Monica and gently guided her toward the door.

We walked hand in hand down the long concourse toward our boarding gate. We could see the two men walking a short distance in front of us. They were going to the same gate.

"Looks like those two are going to be on the same flight as we are," Monica said with a grin.

"Imagine that," I replied with a grin and a slight squeeze of her hand.

After boarding the plane, we found ourselves just three rows back of the two men. I watched the two men as they settled in. They where trying very hard not to let us know that they had any interest in us, almost too hard.

It was a nice day and the flight was expected to be smooth. Before long, we were airborne. I continued to hold Monica's hand as I closed my eyes and tipped back to relax. Monica also tipped back to relax. Since the two men had tried to make it look like they were not following us, I didn't think there was any reason that I couldn't relax and enjoy the flight.

I didn't sleep. I simple closed my eyes and began to think about what we were getting into. Of course there was no way for us to know, but it was a good idea to be prepared for anything. The one thing that I was convinced of was that the disk that Jeff was to deliver to General Dynamics must have been very important. If it was not important, why was Games Unlimited going to such lengths to make sure we were followed?

It suddenly occurred to me that I had come to assume that these two men worked for Games Unlimited. Past experience had taught me that one should never assume anything. Just because they started following us from there, didn't necessarily mean that they worked for Games Unlimited. They could be working for almost any one. At this point in time, I wasn't sure who they were, or who they worked for.

Regardless of who they were, they must have had a pretty good idea that we were looking for Jeff. I had to ask myself how they knew Jeff was missing? The more I thought about it, the more convinced I became that the phone lines in Jeff's office, and probably his house, had been tapped. We knew that Sharon had called Jeff's secretary and told her that Jeff had not checked into his hotel. Sharon had told us that much.

We knew that Sharon had told Miss Marshall that we would probably be coming by to see her. Again, Miss Marshall told us that.

All they had to do was wait at the Games Unlimited building for us to show up. When we showed up at Games Unlimited, they knew just what we were doing there. It made it easy for them to find us, too easy.

There was no way of knowing for sure what Miss Marshall had told Sharon, but it was clear that she had not told Sharon about Jeff's side trip to Knollwoods Resort and Casino to test his Blackjack system. The one thing that was clear was that someone must have had a pretty good idea what was said between Sharon and Miss Marshall over the phone. That meant that either Sharon's phone or Miss Marshall's phone could have been taped.

The more I thought about it, the more I wondered what was going on. Miss Marshall seemed to be sincerely worried about Jeff. I got the impression that it was more than one would expect from a company secretary. She seemed afraid to talk to us, but at the same time afraid not to. She told us about Jeff's planned side trip that no one else seemed to know anything about. It caused me to briefly wonder what the relationship between Jeff and Miss Marshall really was.

Then there was Games Unlimited. With all their security, and the fact that we were being followed, gave credence to my thought that this was some serious business we were getting involved in. The disk that Jeff was supposed to deliver could be anything from an upgrade for some basic computer program for General Dynamics to some top-secret military program. I tended to lean toward some top-secret military program, if for no other reason than it would keep me on my toes.

I had to wonder how much Jeff really knew. Was he just a courier who really didn't know what he was delivering? That was certainly a possibility. There was also the possibility that he not only knew what he was delivering, but that he had a hand in developing it. After all, he was a computer whiz. He also worked for the company that had apparently created the software disk in the first place. It made me wonder if maybe his job as Director of Games might be some sort of cover for something else more secretive or sensitive in nature.

My mind was filled with a lot of unanswered questions. The one thing that I was convinced of was that none of my questions were going to be answered by talking to the two men who were following us. I was sure that they wouldn't tell us anything.

I felt Monica lightly squeeze my hand. I opened my eyes and looked over at her.

"I think someone wants to talk to you," she said then turned her head a little and looked past me.

I turned and saw one of the men that had been following us standing next to his seat looking at me. It surprised me a little that they were willing to acknowledge us. But then, they had probably figured out by now that we already knew they were there.

The man nodded his head and looked toward the back of the airplane. I quickly realized that he wanted to meet with me at the back of the plane. Maybe I had been wrong. Maybe they were willing to talk to me, after all. I doubted that he would be willing to tell me very much, though. The only way to find out was to talk to them.

I nodded that I understood and stood up. As I moved to the back of the plane, I noticed that there were two rows of seats that were not occupied. When I looked back at the man, he casually pointed to a seat. I moved into the row and sat down. He quickly moved in beside me.

"What can I do for you?" I asked wanting him to start the discussion.

"My name is Kenneth Boyer. I'm the head of security at Games Unlimited. I know who you are, Mr. McCord."

"I'm sure you do. Do you mind telling me why you find it necessary to follow us?"

"I'm sure you already know the answer to that. Mr. Holcome has disappeared. We want to know what happened to him, just as much as you do, maybe more."

"What makes you think anything happened to him?"

"I don't want to get into a game of words with you, Mr. McCord. I've been on the phone to our home office. They've agree with me that it would be in our best interest to have you working for us, rather then for us to try to find Mr. Holcome ourselves. We do not have that kind of experience. I am told that you are a very good investigator. What I'm saying is, we would like to have you working for us."

"If I'm working for someone, I want to know who I'm working for and what it is they expect of me," I said as I looked him in the eye.

"You would be working directly for Games Unlimited. I would be your contact," he replied.

"Well, that clears up part of it. What about the rest?"

"We expect you to find Mr. Holcome."

"Then what?"

"I don't understand."

"I think you do. You are not as much interested in finding Mr. Holcome as you are in finding out what happened to the disk that he was supposed to deliver to General Dynamics. Am I right?"

He paused for a moment before he asked, "How do you know about that?"

The sound of his voice and the look in his eyes didn't convince me that he was as surprised as he tried to make me believe. There was no doubt in my mind that he knew that I knew about the disk long before I mentioned it.

"Like you said, I'm a good investigator," I replied with a grin.

I could see that he was thinking hard. Probably trying to decide how much he should tell me while wondering how much I already knew.

"You are partly right. I doubt that you will believe me, but we do want to know what happened to Mr. Holcome. And you are correct when you say we are interested in finding that disk. But more importantly, we are interested in who has the disk now."

"You think that someone else already has the disk?"

"Yes. At least it's a strong possibility."

"Well, if someone other than Jeff has the disk, it's too late. They certainly would have copied it, or at the least read it by now."

"If they try to copy it, it will destroy itself. The information on the disk is in code and can only be read by a computer that knows the code. General Dynamics is the only one that has the codes, and Games Unlimited, of course."

"Well, I think you have a problem?"

"What do you mean?"

"If someone else has the disk, there's a good chance that they also have a computer that can access the information on it, or can at least figure out what the code is to get the information from the disk. That would most likely mean that there is someone at either Games Unlimited or General Dynamics that can retrieve the information on that disk."

"What you're saying is that we have someone on the inside that wants that information?" Boyer asked.

"I doubt that they want the information as much as they want the money that the information will buy," I suggested.

"I see your point," he replied thoughtfully. "But I get the impression that you don't think Mr. Holcome took it."

"I don't really know Jeff all that well, but what I do know about him makes me wonder if he's your man. At this point, I have no reason to believe that he would be the one selling the disk. Do you have something that would convince me otherwise?"

"Nothing solid, but I do know that he likes to gamble," he admitted.

"You think gambling is reason enough for him to want to steal the disk and sell it?"

"It could be. It would provide him with money to feed his gambling habit," Boyer said.

"As far as I know, Jeff might gamble a little from time to time, but I seriously doubt that he's a compulsive gambler," I said wondering if he might be.

"At this point, I think the first thing we need to do is find Jeff. Right now, I plan to continue following his every move until I find out what happened to him," I added.

"Does that mean you will work for us?" Boyer asked.

"It means that I will talk it over with my partner. If we decide to work for you, we will expect full compensation for our time and effort. If not, you can bet that I will lose you within an hour after this plane touches down in Connecticut. I'll let you know our decision before we get off the plane."

I got up and left him sitting there with his jaw hanging open. I was sure he didn't know what to think. I was also sure that he believed that I could lose him that easily.

As I sat down next to Monica, I could see that she could hardly wait to find out what Boyer and I had talked about. I took the next few minutes to tell her about my conversation with Kenneth Boyer.

"What do you think we should do?" she asked.

"I think we might as well work with them. It just might be helpful to have them on our side in case we run into trouble."

"I agree, but they might also get in the way. They might not be on our side, either," Monica said in her usual way of casually pointing out that I might have overlooked something.

In this case, I had not overlooked the possibility that they might not be on our side. What I was looking at was that if they thought we were working with them, I might be able to control some of what they do and I might be able to keep better tabs on them.

"That's possible. I think I can convince them to do as I tell them. Kenneth Boyer seems like a smart man. He also knows his limits. Trying to find someone is a little out of his realm of expertise, so he says. I think I can get him to depend on us and to stay out of our way, at least for a little while, at the same time."

"Okay. If you think it will be better to have him on our side, than I'm all for it," Monica said with a smile.

I squeezed her hand and leaned over and kissed her lightly on the lips. I then looked around the corner of my seat and saw Kenneth still sitting in the back of the plane where I had left him.

"I guess I better put his mind to rest. I'll work out an agreement with him."

I squeezed her hand again, then stood up and walked back to where Kenneth Boyer was sitting. The expression on his face made it clear to me that he was hopeful that we would work for them, but that he wasn't sure of our decision. I sat down beside him.

"I talked to my partner. We have agreed to work for you if we can agree on terms."

"I'm sure we can. What are your terms?"

"We want you to find a nice motel or hotel in the area and stay put while we follow our leads. We don't want you on our tail. We have no way of knowing if you are being tailed. If you are, we don't want you leading them to us."

"I understand. You're the expert."

"We also want five hundred dollars a day, plus expenses. That includes reimbursement for this flight, car rentals, hotels, meals, everything."

"No problem."

"Then we have a deal?"

"Yes, we have a deal, Mr. McCord."

"By the way, leaving us to do our job means that all of your security people leave us alone."

"I understand. How will I get in touch with you?"

"You won't. I'll get in touch with you. You have a cell phone?"

"Yes."

"I want the number. Don't go anywhere without that phone. I may need to get in touch with you at a moment's notice."

"Where would you like us to stay?" Boyer asked.

"When you get off the plane, rent a car and go to Groton. Find a nice motel and wait for me to call you."

"Okay. I'll be waiting for your call," he said as he handed me his business card with a cell phone number on it.

"Something you should know. We are being met at the airport by the head of security from General Dynamics."

"Great. Ah, you get off the plane and meet them. We will follow you off the plane, but act as if you don't know us. I want to get a look at them so I know who I'm dealing with."

"Okay. Mr. McCord, I'm glad that you are working with us."

"Yeah. Just make sure you keep your end of the bargain."

I stood up and walked back to my assigned seat. Boyer's last comment caused me to wonder. Was he really glad that we had joined forces with him or was he saying that in an effort to convince me that he would work with me? Only time would answer that question.

Over the years I had learned to be careful whom I trusted. When it came to investigations, I had learned not to make judgments based on what a person says, but to look for the facts. People often proved to be wrong. Boyer seemed sincere and straightforward enough, but there was something in the way he looked at me that caused me to wonder about him. Maybe it was that he seemed just a little too agreeable to what I asked of him. Then again, maybe it was my paranoia.

I also wondered if Games Unlimited would follow through on our agreement. Since I didn't know who was pulling the strings back at Games Unlimited Headquarters, I felt it would be prudent for me to continue to watch Boyer as well as my own back.

"What's wrong?" Monica asked as I sat down.

"Nothing."

"Did he agree to our terms?"

"Yes. Yes, he did. And without a moment's hesitation."

"Then what's the worried look for?"

"I'm not sure. I sort of trust Boyer, but I don't know how much control he has over this operation of his to find Jeff."

"Is that a problem?"

"It could be."

Monica sat back in her seat and stared straight ahead. I could tell by the look on her face that she was as concerned about all of this as I was. Maybe that was my fault. I had some doubts and I had expressed them without any proof.

We would be landing soon. We would have to keep an eye out for anyone following us. Neither of us knew what to expect at the airport. We didn't know who might be waiting for us. We weren't expecting anyone, which made it even more unnerving.

I sat back and listened to the changing sounds of the plane as it prepared for a landing at the Springfield-Hartford

Airport. I reviewed in my mind the list of places that Jeff was planning to go when he arrived. Although there were a number of places that Jeff was scheduled to be, the one that was not on his schedule was the one that stuck in my mind. I had to wonder why he had not included the Knollwoods Resort and Casino on the itinerary that he had given Sharon.

If Jeff was a compulsive gambler, the Casino would be a likely place for him to go. It was also the most likely place for him to go to test his system for winning at Blackjack. The fact that he was planning on doing some gambling was not reason enough for me to believe that he was a compulsive gambler.

The fact that Boyer knew Jeff gambled was not all that interesting or important, either. After all, if he was head of security at Games Unlimited, it was his job to know about the people employed there, including their habits, both good and bad.

I was sure that if Jeff had been considered a compulsive gambler, he would not have been employed in such a security sensitive place. He certainly would not have been given any kind of sensitive material to deliver outside the confines of the Games Unlimited building, let alone half way across the country. I began to think that I really needed to find out more about Jeff and his habits for myself.

CHAPTER FOUR

As soon as the plane had taxied to a stop at the gate, almost everyone stood up. Monica and I remained seated to avoid the rush of people trying to get off the plane all at once. We were in no hurry to get off the plane. I wanted Boyer to get off first, so he could find the men who were supposed to meet him; and so we could get a chance to see who it was that he was meeting.

I watched as Boyer and his partner stood up. While standing in the aisle waiting for people to clear out, he looked back over his shoulder at me. We made eye contact, and I had to wonder if he was going to keep our agreement or not. I'm sure that he was probably wondering the same thing about me.

Monica and I waited until most of the passengers had cleared out before we stepped out in the aisle and started working our way to the front of the plane. Once inside the terminal, we started toward the baggage claim area for our luggage.

Almost as soon as we were out of the secure area of the airport, we saw Boyer and his partner standing off to the side. They were greeting two other men, just as Boyer had said they would. I took note of the other two men as we walked past. One of them was tall with dark hair and dark eyes and he wore a dark suit. There was a slight bulge under the left side of his suit coat. It was clear to me that he was carrying a gun. I remembered Boyer telling me that he was to meet the head of security for General Dynamics. I took a good look at him. I wanted to remember what he looked like just in case I should run across him again.

The other man was smaller, but just as well dressed. His dark brown hair was neatly trimmed, as was his mustache. He seemed to be just standing there listening to the conversation after introductions. I got the impression that he seemed rather comfortable. It was almost as if he knew he was where he belonged. Something about him gave me the impression that he might just be a hired gun. I don't know why that thought crossed my mind, but it did. Maybe it was the way he stood. He seemed self-confident, alert and aware of his surroundings. Although he was not very tall, he looked as if he was very capable of taking care of himself. It bothered me just a little. For some reason that I couldn't put my finger on, he didn't strike me as the security type. He reminded me more of a bodyguard than a security guard. I got the feeling that he could be very dangerous. He was someone to be leery of when close by

Monica and I walked on by toward the baggage claim area. We retrieved our baggage and went directly to the car rental counter. Standing behind the counter was a nice looking young woman with a pleasant smile.

"May I help you," she asked in a pleasant voice.

"Yes. We would like to rent a car. We would also like a little information, please," I said.

"Certainly. I'll do what I can to help."

"I need to know if you were working on this counter at about this same time on Monday?"

"Yes. Yes, I was," she replied, the look on her face showing that she was not sure why I would ask such a question.

"Do you remember renting a car to a Mr. Jeffery Holcome from Chicago?"

"Is there something wrong?" she asked as a worried look came over her face.

"No. There is nothing wrong. I just need to know if he rented a car from you?"

"Yes," she replied, looking a little confused.

"How did he appear to you?"

"I'm sorry, but I don't understand. What do you mean?"

"Did he appear upset, nervous, restless, or was he calm and relaxed?" I asked trying not to influence her answer.

"Well, now that you mention it, he seemed to be in kind of a hurry. You know, like he was late for an appointment or something."

"Did he seem upset, maybe a little on edge?"

"I guess you could say that. He kept looking around as if he was looking for someone."

"Did he look like he was hoping to meet someone?"

"No. I don't think so," she said thoughtfully. "It was more like he was hoping not to meet someone, if you know what I mean?"

"Yes, I think I do."

The fact that he seemed nervous didn't surprise me that much. If Jeff thought that the disk he was carrying had some important military secret on it, he was bound to be nervous. And if what the rental clerk had said was correct, I was convinced that Jeff knew what was on the disk, or at least he had a pretty good idea what was on it.

There were so many unanswered questions going through my mind that I missed what the young woman said next. I heard Monica respond for me.

"That would be fine."

"Your car will be in lot six, space fourteen," the young woman said as she handed Monica the keys.

"Thank you," I said as I turned and started to walk away from the counter with Monica.

"Oh, one more thing," the young woman called out.

I stopped and turned around to see what more she had to say.

"After Mr. Holcome left here, he went right to the phone over there and made a call," she said as she pointed toward a bank of payphones. "He seemed very much relieved after he made the call. You know, not so uptight, more relaxed."

"Thank you. Thank you for your help," I replied, then turned back around and walked away with Monica.

"What's going on?" Monica asked, her concern showing on her face.

"I don't know, but I think Jeff knew what he had on that disk, or at least he suspected what was on it."

"Do you think it frightened him?"

"Everything sure points to it. What other reason would he have for being so nervous?"

"Well, maybe he was wondering what his wife would think of him going off to gamble," Monica suggested.

"Why would that worry him here? There was no possibility that she would be around."

"He didn't tell her that he was going to go gambling. Maybe he felt guilty about it. That makes some men feel like they are cheating on their wives, even if it is not really cheating in the common meaning of the term," Monica suggested.

"I guess you could be right, but what about the phone call? The clerk said that he wasn't so uptight after he called someone," I reminded her.

"Maybe it was to whoever he was to take the disk to."

"That could be, but we won't know until we find Jeff and asked him."

We took our baggage and started to walk out to where the rental car could be found. As we passed through the door, I saw Boyer and his partner get into a black Chevy Tahoe along with the two men that we had seen him with in the airport. The vehicle was typical of those used by the U.S. Government. I wished that I could have seen the license plate so that I could have been sure.

That got me to thinking. If the government was involved with this, then the disk that disappeared with Jeff was of some value to the government. If that was the case, it was probably top secret in nature.

"Here it is," Monica said as she pointed to a silver gray Ford sedan.

She unlocked the trunk and opened it. We put our bags in, then got in the car. I sat behind the wheel for several minutes just thinking. Monica was kind enough to sit quietly and not disturb my thoughts for several minutes.

"What did you do with that itinerary of Jeff's?"

"It's right here," Monica replied as she pulled the paper out of her purse. "What are you looking for?"

"I want to check and make sure that we are following Jeff's every step. I've got this uneasy feeling that I've overlooked something."

I took the paper and looked it over. There it was in plain sight. It had been right under my nose all the time. I hadn't noticed it the first time I looked at it, but it was clear now. Jeff had arrived a full three days before the conference on computer games was to begin. I had to wonder why he needed so much lead time. It certainly wouldn't take him three days to deliver the disk to General Dynamics.

His secretary had told us that he was planning on testing some new game, and that he went early to do just that. If he wanted to keep that from Sharon, he wasn't doing a very good job of it. He must have known that Sharon would call him at the hotel in Hartford the same day he arrived. She would know right away that he was not where he said he would be.

I remembered when I was married to her. She would call me if I wasn't home when she thought I should be. There was no reason for me to think that she had changed any.

That thought caused me to wonder if Jeff had ever gone out of town without her before? They had been married for less than two years. Then it hit me. He would not know that she would call him every day he was gone. He was her idea of the perfect husband. He was probably always home in the evening, and always home in time for dinner. He would not have gotten the complaints from her for not being home on time, working late, or having to stay out on a stakeout until the wee hours of the morning.

"I'll bet that Sharon doesn't know about Jeff's gambling," I said as I looked over at Monica.

"What are you talking about?"

"Jeff is Sharon's idea of the perfect husband, always home on time and never late. Jeff was planning on doing some gambling before the conference. His secretary told us that much. I'd be willing to bet that he never expected Sharon to call him at the hotel. He probably figured he had a couple of days before the conference to test his system without anyone being the wiser. And from the looks of his itinerary, he planned on a couple of days of gambling after the conference as well."

"Did Sharon keep close tabs on you when you were married to her?" Monica asked.

"Oh, you wouldn't believe. If I wasn't where she expected me to be, she was on the phone to everyone she could think of in an effort to find out where I was. And when I didn't get home when she thought I should, she would give me the third degree about where I had been, who I had seen, and what I had been doing. She had this compulsive need to know where I was all the time."

"Jealousy?"

"I don't know if it was jealousy or her own insecurity or what. But it was one of the major things that caused our divorce. It was like she didn't trust me."

"Where to now?"

"Jeff's secretary said that he planned to go to Knollwoods Resort and Casino. I think we should go there. My guess is that he went directly to the Casino from here," I said as I folded up Jeff's itinerary and handed it back to Monica.

"Wasn't he supposed to deliver that disk to General Dynamics as soon as he arrived?" Monica asked.

"I don't know. We assume that he was, but as far as we know he never got there. We got that much out of Mr. Boyer."

"Do you think Jeff was in so much of a hurry to try out his Blackjack system that he would delay delivering the disk to General Dynamics? After all, it seems that the disk tended to make him rather nervous," Monica reminded me.

"You are probably right, if it was the disk that made him nervous."

"What are you getting at?"

"Think about this. Jeff arrives at about the same time we did, only on Monday. He gets his baggage, rents his car and starts off to Groton. By the time he gets close to Groton, he realizes that it is getting pretty late. He wants to get rid of the disk, but he is anxious to try out his system at the Blackjack tables. So rather than arrive past normal office hours at General Dynamics to make his delivery, he decides to stop off at Knollwoods Resort and Casino for the night. Probably with the idea of delivering the disk first thing in the morning," I explained.

"I guess that makes some sense, if he didn't know how important that disk was. But what do you think happened to him from there?" Monica asked.

"I don't have any idea. We know that he didn't go to his hotel in Hartford. I think we need to find out if he went to Knollwoods Resort and Casino."

Monica nodded her head in agreement. I reached down, turned the ignition key and started the car. I pulled out of the parking lot. With Monica using the map that we got with the papers on the rented car, she directed me to Interstate 91, then south toward Hartford. We took highway 2 from Hartford to Colchester, then highway 85 to Groton.

We arrived in Groton at about six-thirty in the evening, Eastern Standard Time. By arriving at that hour we did confirm my suspicions that Jeff would have arrived too late to make his deliver during normal working hours.

It took us a little while to find our way to Knollwoods Resort and Casino. When we arrived, we were lucky enough to find that they had a room available. We signed in and took our baggage to our room.

"Why didn't you ask the desk clerk if Jeff was registered here?" Monica asked.

"I don't want the desk clerk to accidentally tell Jeff that we are here. I want to check around a little first. Besides, if we start asking too many questions too soon, they might get security involved and I'm not ready for that. I don't want to have to explain anything to security. After we look around a little, if nothing shows up I'll want to talk to the head of security in the morning."

"Oh. Well, if you don't have any other plans, maybe we could get something to eat?" Monica suggested.

"That sounds like a good idea," I agreed.

I took Monica's hand and we left our room. We took the elevator down to the casino level and got off. We went into the first place we found that we could get a good meal. It was the Cedars Steakhouse Grill. We sat down to an excellent steak dinner.

"Do you think that Jeff might still be here?" Monica asked.

"I suppose he could be. According to his itinerary, the conference doesn't start until Thursday evening with a dinner and the opening speeches."

"Why didn't we just wait for him at his hotel in Hartford if the conference starts on Thursday evening?"

"Because someone is already missing him."

"Sure, Sharon. But she didn't know that he had three days before the conference," Monica said.

"No, not Sharon. Well, yes, she is missing him. But I'm more concerned with the others who are missing him. No one just jumps in on a missing person this quickly unless there's something very important involved. From what was said, or at least hinted at by Boyer, I get the idea that Jeff didn't show up at General Dynamics with the disk the morning after he landed. So they immediately started looking for him. That tells me that someone is worried about that disk."

"Are you sure about the disk?" Monica asked.

After giving it a moment of thought, I replied, "No. But at this point I have nothing else to go on. Boyer even hinted that something was missing. My best guess is the disk. I'm open to suggestions. Do you have a better idea?"

"No, and I see what you mean."

We finished our meal with little conversation. I don't know what was on Monica's mind, but I was wondering if Jeff was still here. After dinner we walked around to get a little acquainted with the casinos and the layout of the resort. It wasn't long before we realized that there were no gaming tables in the area known as the Great Cedar Casino.

Monica and I took our time as we walked around and watched the players at the slot machines. Some of the customers were holding their own, some were losing and a few were winning a little here and there.

"Do you see him anywhere?" Monica asked.

"No. There are a couple of places where they have gaming tables. Since Blackjack is a table game, let's check them out."

With Monica's hand still in mine, we left the area and walked toward another area called the Grand Pequot Casino. We walked around to the area where the gaming tables were located. I was especially interested in the Blackjack tables. We saw no sign of Jeff anywhere, but it would not have been hard to miss him in such a big place. There were so many tables and so many people milling around that it was almost like trying to find a needle in a haystack.

"Let's try one of the other areas," I suggested.

"Okay."

We backtracked along Pequot Trail, one of the long hallways to the Great Cedar Casino. We walked through the casino and came out on the hallway called Rainmaker Trail. We came out just short of Rainmaker Casino.

After wandering around the gaming tables and having no luck finding Jeff there either, I began to think that the only way we were going to find him was to contact the casino's security. I had no idea how much help they would be willing to give us. The only thing I could do was to ask.

"I think we should head back to our room," I said.

"This is almost hopeless trying to find him in here," Monica said with a sigh of disappointment.

"I know. I think we should talk to security in the morning. Maybe they will help us find him."

"Do you think they will help?" Monica asked.

"I don't know, but it's worth a try."

"Maybe we should check with the desk clerk and see if he even has a room here," Monica suggested.

"I hadn't even thought that he might not stay here. It's probably a good idea to check with the evening desk clerk on our way back to our room. We're never going to find him in here by ourselves," I agreed.

Monica and I started back toward the elevator that would take us to our room. It was interesting just looking around at all the people as they went about their business. Some were just walking around amazed at the size and beauty of the place, some were playing the slot machines, and some just standing around watching others play.

We went to the front desk of the hotel. There were two people behind the desk, a woman that looked like she might be in her mid-thirties, and a man who was older. The man saw us first. He approached us with a smile.

"May I help you?" he asked pleasantly.

"I was wondering if you could tell me if you have a Jeffrey Holcome registered here?" I asked.

"Let me check, sir," the man said as he stepped over in front of a computer.

I glanced at Monica, then at the woman who was standing off to the side. The woman was looking at me. I got the impression that she might know something. I can't really say what it was about her that made me think that, but I did.

"I'm sorry, sir. Mr. Holcome checked out a little while ago."

"Then he was here?"

"Yes, sir," the clerk replied.

"What time did he check out?"

"Ah, it says here that he checked out at eight-thirty-five this evening," he replied as he looked at the screen of the monitor, then turned to look at me.

"Eight-thirty-five this evening?"

"Yes, sir. It seems that you just missed him."

"Yes. It would seem so."

I had to wonder why he would check out at that hour. It made no sense to me for him to check out tonight. He didn't have to be in Hartford until Thursday evening.

"Is there anything else I can help you with, sir?" the man asked.

He seemed puzzled by my reaction.

"No. No, thank you."

I took Monica's hand and turned away from the desk. We walked toward the elevator that would take us up to the floor that our room was located on. We found ourselves in the elevator alone.

"Why would he check out in the evening?" Monica asked.

"That's what I was wondering."

"Do you suppose he found out that his system didn't work and lost all his money?" Monica asked.

"It's possible, but why would he leave now? He certainly would have paid for his room already. And as far as we know, he still has the disk. I would think he would have waited until morning and deliver it."

"Maybe he doesn't have it anymore," Monica suggested.

"If he doesn't have it, what happened to it?"

Monica just shrugged her shoulders. The thought that he might not have the disk had crossed my mind. If he didn't have it, than who did? And where was he now?

"You know, we haven't been in contact with Boyer since we left the airport. I wonder if Jeff might have delivered the disk after we landed?" Monica asked.

"I'm sure they were still missing the disk when we landed or they wouldn't have been waiting for Boyer to show up."

"But maybe, just maybe, he turned in the disk between the time we landed and now."

Monica had a good point. For all we know, he could have turned it in between the time we last talked to Boyer and now, and then gone to Hartford for his conference.

"Why don't you call Boyer and ask him? He should know if it was delivered," Monica suggested.

"I think I will."

As soon as we got to our room, I sat down at the table next to the bed and picked up the phone. After getting an outside line, I dialed the number that Boyer had given me. The phone only rang twice before it was answered.

"Hello?"

"Boyer?"

"Yeah."

"This is McCord. Where are you?"

"I'm in a motel here in Groton. That's what you wanted."

"Good. I need to know if Jeff has turned in the disk yet?"

Boyer hesitated before he replied. I thought I could hear voices in the background.

"No, not yet. Why?"

"When was the last time you checked with General Dynamics?" I asked ignoring his question.

"Just about thirty minutes ago."

"What did they tell you?"

Again, he hesitated before he replied. This time I was sure that I heard voices in the background. My first thought was that he had the television on.

"They said they still didn't have it."

"Did they say if they had heard from Jeff at all?"

The voices in the background were still there, only this time I didn't feel like it was a television. I couldn't make out what was being said, but there was definitely someone else in the room with Boyer. I got the impression that someone might be coaching him on what to tell me.

"No, not a word. Have you had any luck in finding him?"

"No, not yet anyway."

"Where are you?"

That was the one question that I was not prepared to answer at this time. I sort of trusted Boyer, but I had some serious doubts about whether he was still in charge. If the head of security for General Dynamics was involved, there was little chance that Boyer would be able to do anything without them listening in and without their instructions.

"I've got to go. I'll call you again later," I said then hung up the phone before Boyer had a chance to say anything more.

"What did he say?"

"It's what he didn't say that bothers me."

"What do you mean?"

"There were at least two other people in the room with him. I could hear them. I couldn't understand what they were saying, but it was clear to me that they were there. They may even have been prompting Boyer on what to say to me."

"Who do you think they are?"

"Probably the men we saw Boyer meet at the airport and Boyer's partner."

"You think they are trying to find out where we are?"

"I'm sure of it. I'm also sure that they think we know more than we do. If that's the case, they're going to be looking for us as much as for Jeff. Boyer as much as said it on the plane. He needed us to find Jeff. When we lost them at the airport, they lost their life line to Jeff."

"Now what?"

"Now we get a good night's sleep and start over in the morning. We will start by talking to the Chief of Security. I'm not sure where it will lead, but we don't have any other leads at the moment," I explained.

"Well, since there's nothing we can do 'til morning," Monica said with a sexy grin on her face.

"I didn't say there was nothing we could do," I said interrupting her.

"Oh. And just what do you have in mind?"

"I see no sense in wasting this beautiful room. I was thinking that we could take a nice warm shower, then spend a little time together on that king-size bed," I suggested.

"Now that sounds like something I might really enjoy. I take it you meant for us to shower together?"

"Of course. There's no sense wasting all that water by taking separate showers."

"Oh, I agree," she replied playfully with a big grin.

"Shall we?" I asked as I stood up and reached out my hand to her.

"Of course," she replied in that sexy voice of hers that I had come to enjoy.

I took her hand and led her into the dressing area. After we had undressed each other, I leaned into the shower and turned on the water. As soon as it was warm enough, I took her hand and stepped into the shower.

I gently pulled Monica close to me. She stepped up and put her hands on my shoulders. I slid my hands around her narrow waist and drew her up against me. She tipped her head back and looked up at me.

“I love you,” she whispered as I leaned down until our lips met.

As we kissed, she slid her arms around behind my neck and pressed her body against me. The feel of her naked body against mine as we kissed washed away all thoughts of anything but her from my mind. She had that affect on me, especially at times like this.

After a long passionate kiss, I leaned back and looked down at her as I took the bar of soap from the soap tray. She smiled at me then turned around. I began washing her smooth beautiful back from her shoulders down to the small of her back. She sighed softly as I slipped my hands around, cupped her firm breasts in my soapy hands and drew her back against me as I kissed her neck.

After some heavy necking and some serious touching, we washed each other and got out of the shower. After drying each other with the big soft towels generously provided by the Knollwoods Resort, I led Monica to the bed and pulled back the covers for her. We climbed into bed and wrapped ourselves in each other's arms.

After some very heavy necking on the oversize bed, we made love to each other. It was a time of eagerness and desire for each other that when mixed together grew into one night of passion. Our time of passion was followed by hours of peaceful sleep.

CHAPTER FIVE

I thought I could hear the sound of someone knocking on the door to our room, but I wasn't sure. I was only half awakened by the noise and not fully conscious of what I was hearing. It was Monica's gentle touch and the sound of her soft voice that brought me out of my sleep and into the real world.

"Nick, I think there's someone at the door," she said, the sound of sleep still in her voice.

"It better not be housekeeping at this hour," I said as I turned and looked at the clock on the bedside table.

Again, there was a knock on the door. Only this time it was louder, much louder.

"Just a minute," I called out as I swung my legs over the side of the bed and sat up.

I got up and pulled on my pants. I zipped up my fly as I walked to the door. I looked through the peephole in the door. There were two men standing in front of the door. One was in a suit while the other was in some kind of uniform. The one in the uniform looked like he might be a security guard for the resort.

"What is it?"

"My name is Bradford, Samuel Bradford," the one in the suit said. "I'm head of security here at Knollwoods, Mr. McCord. I would like to have a word with you, if I may."

I wasn't sure what was going on, but this was the man that I was planning on talking with this morning. Not having expected him, I had to wonder why he had come to me.

Only after looking back at Monica to make sure that she was covered, did I open the door.

"What can I do for you, Mr. Bradford?" I asked as I stood in the doorway blocking him from seeing inside the room.

"I understand that you were asking questions about a Mr. Holcome, Jeffrey Holcome, at the desk last night. Is that correct?"

"Yes," I replied, still wondering what he wanted.

"I would like to talk to you about him, if you don't mind."

"Okay, but it will have to wait until we get dressed?"

"Certainly. We can talk in my office, if that is okay with you."

"That would be fine. It will be just a few minutes."

"This guard will wait here in the hall and escort you to my office."

"Sure. We'll be ready in a few minutes."

Mr. Bradford nodded, then turned and walked away. I shut the door and returned to the room.

"Who was that?"

"It was Mr. Samuel Bradford, Chief of Security here at Knollwoods."

"Oh. What does he want?"

"He wants to talk to us about Jeff."

"How did he know we are looking for Jeff?"

"I'm not sure, but I think the woman at the desk last night probably told him. When we asked about Jeff, I noticed that she seemed to take an interest us."

"I wonder why?"

"I don't know, but I think you better get dressed. We have a meeting with the Chief of Security in his office as soon as possible. Maybe we'll get lucky and get some answers."

I watched as Monica sat up on the side of the bed and the sheet slid down off her lovely body. She was the most beautiful woman I could ever imagine. I watched her as she stood up and walked into the bathroom. She moved with the grace and smoothness of a goddess, and the shape of her body was in itself a work of art.

While Monica was in the bathroom, I brushed my teeth and shaved. When she came out I was getting dressed.

"What would you like me to wear?" she asked.

"Anything comfortable," I replied.

"I'm comfortable in nothing with you," she replied playfully.

"That's nice and I like you that way, but I think clothes would be appropriate this morning," I said as I grinned at her.

"Okay," she said with a teasing smile.

Monica dressed in slacks and a blouse that were very nice looking on her. As I finished dressing, I couldn't help but wonder what she saw in me. I'm as plain as they come, and she was as beautiful a woman as I'd ever seen.

Once we were finished dressing, I walked to the door and waited for her to join me. We were ready. I was sure that the guard outside our door was getting tired of waiting and growing impatient for us to show up. I opened the door and let Monica go out first.

After checking the door to make sure it locked, we followed the guard to the elevator. The guard never said a word until we got to Mr. Bradford's office, even then he didn't speak to us. He simply told the woman at the desk that we were there. She took us on into Mr. Bradford's office.

Mr. Bradford was sitting behind a large oak desk. When we entered, he immediately stood up to greet us.

"Please, have a seat at the table," he said as he came around from behind the desk.

"This is Monica Barnhart, my partner."

"Welcome to Knollwoods Resort and Casino," he replied.

"What is it you wanted to see us about?" I asked in an effort to get right to the point.

"Before we get into that, could I offer you something for breakfast? Anything you like."

Monica looked at me and I shrugged my shoulders. She then turned and looked back at Mr. Bradford and smiled.

"Black coffee and a Danish would be nice," she said.

"And you, sir?"

"That would be fine," I replied.

While Bradford gave his secretary instructions over the phone, I pulled back a chair for Monica and waited for her to sit down. I then sat down beside her.

"It was brought to my attention by the clerk at the desk yesterday evening that you had inquired about Mr. Holcome," he said as he sat down across the table from us. "May I ask why?"

"I'm sure you have a number of people who ask about guests. They are either friends, relatives or someone who saw someone they thought they knew and wanted to find out if they were staying here," I replied.

I was curious as to why he wanted to know what our interest in Jeff might be. I wouldn't think that the head of security would show this much interest in what should have looked like a routine inquiry about a guest, unless there was something wrong.

"Which are you, Mr. McCord?"

"Let's just say that I know Mr. Holcome."

"Okay, let's say that. I would still like to know why you are interested in finding him."

The way he phrased his question interested me.

"What makes you think we are trying to find him?"

"You asked about him."

"You are showing a lot of interest in Mr. Holcome yourself, more than one might expect. Why is that?"

"It's my job."

"What do you say that we quit playing games? Of all the guests here, you pick out this one to ask me questions about. Why? What do you know about him that you're not telling us?

"I'm not ready to divulge that just yet."

"In that case, I think this conversation is over," I said as I pushed back my chair and stood up.

"I could have you placed under arrest, Mr. McCord," he threatened, but it seemed like a half-hearted threat.

I put both hands on the table and leaned forward. Looking him right in the eyes I said, "You might be able to do that, but I wouldn't suggest that you try that with me. I don't think you would like the very large lawsuit that would be dropped right in the middle of your big fancy desk."

I straightened up and reached for the back of Monica's chair.

"Wait, please," he said, then looked at me as if he were trying to decide what to do now that I had called his bluff.

"Well?" I asked as I waited for him to make the next move.

"You win, Mr. McCord. Please, sit down."

I was about to ask Mr. Bradford a question, but I heard a light knock on the door. I turned around to see a well-dressed woman carrying a tray. She set the tray on the table, then poured each of us a cup of coffee. When she was done, she left the room. I waited for the door to close before I said anything.

"What do you say that we just start over," I suggested as I sat back down next to Monica. "What is your interest in Jeff Holcome?"

I decided that if he shared what information he might have with me, then I might cooperate with him, at least a little.

"Early this morning, one of our housekeepers went to Mr. Holcome's room. Since he had checked out yesterday evening and we had no immediate need of the room, no one bothered to prepare the room for another guest. This morning, the housekeeper found what looked to her like blood on the sheets and one of the pillowcases, as well as on a towel in the bathroom. The housekeeper said that it looked like there may have been a fight in the room."

What he was saying certainly grabbed my attention. From the look on Monica's face, it had grabbed hers as well.

"Where is this housekeeper now?" I asked.

"She is in my outer office."

"Get her in here, please. I would like to talk to her. By the way, have you notified the police?"

"Not yet. I have no real proof that foul play had taken place. We would rather not bring in the police unless it is necessary."

I nodded that I understood, then took a sip of my coffee. He reached over and picked up the phone. He told his secretary to bring the housekeeper into his office, then hung up.

It wasn't but a couple of minutes before a woman in her mid-fifties came into the room. She was dressed in the uniform of a hotel housekeeper.

"Mr. McCord, this is Maggie Brightwell. She was assigned to the floor where Mr. Holcome's room was located."

"Good morning, Maggie," I said softly.

"Good morning, sir."

She appeared to be a little nervous, but than I couldn't blame her for that. I think Monica could see that she was nervous as well.

"Good morning, Maggie. I'm Monica. Please, sit down."

Monica's voice was soft and pleasant.

Maggie looked at Mr. Bradford for some sign from him that it was okay to sit down. As soon as he motioned toward a chair, she sat down and looked at me.

"Maggie, I want you to tell me what you found in the room that had been occupied by Mr. Holcome," I asked.

"Well, sir. I found what looked like blood on his bed sheets and pillowcases. The room was a mess. It sort of looked like someone had been fighting in there," she replied nervously.

"What makes you think there had been a fight in the room?" Monica asked.

Maggie looked at Mr. Bradford for his approval to answer the question, then back at Monica.

"You may answer their questions freely," Bradford said with a smile.

"The mattress was not straight on the bed, a couple of pillows were on the floor, and the lamp on the table had been knocked over and the bulb was broken. And, of course, there was the blood on the sheets and pillow cases."

"Had you been in the room at any other time while Mr. Holcome was staying here?" I asked.

"Yes, sir. I was in his room yesterday morning to straighten it up for him. He was there."

"He didn't mind you straightening up the room while he was there?"

"No. I offered to come back later, but he said to go ahead and straighten up. He also told me to please do it quietly."

"He stayed in the room the whole time you were there?" Monica asked.

"Yes, Ma'am," she replied.

"What was he doing while you were straightening up his room?" I asked.

"He just sat in one of the chairs at the table. He looked like he was doing something on one of those little computer things."

"You mean a laptop computer?" I asked.

"Yes, sir. I think he was playing some sort of game on it. It looked like a card game."

"Maybe, Blackjack?"

"Yes. That's what he was playing."

"Did he say anything to you while you were there?"

"Yes," she replied as she glanced over at Mr. Bradford. "He got a little upset with me when I tried to move his briefcase from the bed so I could make it. He yelled at me not to touch it. I think he was just worried that I might spill it. It wasn't closed. He apologized for yelling at me, then took the briefcase off the bed and set it on a chair so I could make the bed. When I was finished, he gave me a tip and apologized again for yelling at me."

"Did you happen to see what was in the briefcase?" I asked.

"Not really."

"Can you remember anything in the briefcase?"

"Well," she said thoughtfully. "I remember that there were some papers, and some of those plastic things they use in those computers."

"You mean disks?"

"Yes. I guess that's what they're called. I don't know much about computers."

This gave me the idea that Jeff might still have had the disk everyone was looking for at the time this housekeeper was in his room. However, there was always the very likely possibility that the disks in his briefcase were disks for something else, and not the one he was to deliver to General Dynamics. That thought caused me to wonder if he still had the disk for General Dynamics when Maggie was in his room.

"Do you have any other questions, Mr. McCord?" Sam asked after a long silence.

"Not at the moment. Thank you very much for your help, Maggie. By the way, have you cleaned that room, yet?"

"No, sir. Mr. Bradford said I was to lock the room and leave it just as I found it."

"Very good. Thanks again."

We all sort of waited for Maggie to leave. I sipped my coffee and wondered about the disks. I had no way of knowing if the disks that the housekeeper saw included the disk that Jeff was supposed to deliver to General Dynamics.

Actually, I had no way of knowing if the disks she saw had anything to do with anything. The disks could have been disks for games, or spare backup disks, or for any number of other things. At this point in time there was no way for me to know.

My thoughts were disturbed by the sound of the door closing as Maggie left. I looked over at Monica. She was looking at me. I had to think that she was wondering the same thing that I was.

"Well, Mr. McCord. What do you think?" Sam asked.

"I think I would like to see the room before the police get a chance to look at it," I replied.

"Okay, but I've been cooperative with you. I think it's time for you to cooperate with me. Just who are you?"

"My name is Nick McCord. I'm a former Milwaukee Police Department Homicide Detective, but I'm currently trying to find Jeff Holcome. His wife asked us to try and find him."

"So you are a private investigator, at least for the moment?"

"Sort of. Before I tell you any more, I need your assurance that you will not tell anyone else what I'm about to tell you."

"You have it," he replied as he leaned forward to listen more closely to what I had to say.

I glanced over at Monica. I could see by the look on her face that she was wondering just how much I was going to reveal to this man.

"Mr. Holcome developed a system that he thinks will make him a winner at the Blackjack tables."

"You think he came here to use this system?"

"Well, sort of. As best I can figure out, he came here more to test it. He never has really tested it before, at least as far as we know. We don't even think he knows if it will work," I explained.

"Let me see if I get this straight. You're telling me that he came here to test a system to win at Blackjack?"

"Right. And I think someone is trying to steal it from him," I added.

"That means you think there might have been foul play in his room?"

"Possibly. Is there any way you can find out if he played any Blackjack and if he won at any of the Blackjack tables?"

"Sure. We would have video tapes of him playing."

"Why would you have video tapes of him playing?"

"We video tape the games all the time. It helps us keep an eye out for people who don't want to play fair," he replied with a grin.

"Would they show anyone standing close to him?"

"Yes, they might. That is if they were not too far away."

"I would like to see those tapes, if possible. I'm most interested in seeing who was around him while he was playing."

"I think that can be arranged. It will take a little time to find just the ones with Mr. Holcome on them."

"While you are finding the tapes, I would like to visit Jeff's room.

"Okay. I'll have a guard take you to his room. I'll get started getting the tapes together."

"Great," I said as I stood up.

"Meet me back here in about an hour," Sam said.

I acknowledged him with a nod as I reached for Monica's chair. We left Sam's office and followed the guard to the room that Jeff had been staying in.

We left the guard outside as we went inside the room to look around. The room was a mess just as Maggie had said.

It looked to me as if there might have been a struggle here, but there was no way to tell who was involved and what the outcome might have been.

We still didn't know what happened to Jeff. Had he gotten away, or had he been taken away? Or was he involved at all?

"Be careful what you touch," I reminded Monica. "Take a good look around, though."

I took my time as I looked around the room. The bed reminded me of one where the victim had been dragged off it, but resisted. I slipped the toe of my shoe under a blanket on the floor and pushed it back just a little. There was a piece of cloth under the edge. I bent down and picked it up.

"What do you make of this," I said holding it up so Monica could see it.

"It looks like the kind of material used in rain coats. You know, like a trench coat. It looks like it might be a pocket that was ripped off a coat."

"A tan trench coat," I said. "I wonder if Jeff has such a coat?"

"I don't know."

We returned to looking over the room. Monica went to the closet and began looking in there. I worked my way around the bed looking for any other clues that might have been left behind during a struggle.

I noticed something at the edge of the mattress. I pushed the mattress back a little in order to get a better look. When I did, I found a matchbook. I bent down and picked it up. The matchbook was from Whaler's Inn in Mystic and had several matches missing. The striker on the matchbook indicated that it had been used several times. I quickly looked for an ashtray. I found one on the floor, but it showed no indication that it had been used.

"Monica, do you remember seeing anything when we were at Jeff's home that would indicate that he smoked?"

"No. I'm sure he didn't. I didn't see one single ashtray. Why?" she asked as she came out of the bathroom.

"I found this matchbook on the floor. Did you find anything?"

"I found a towel with blood on it. I would say that a woman used it," Monica said confidently.

"How do you know that?"

"I smelled it. The other towels smell like hotel towels, but the one with blood smells of some kind of cologne. It's a scent that I remember from somewhere, but I can't place it."

"Are you sure?"

"Yes. It's a fairly common cologne. It can be purchased at almost any department store. I just can't think of the name of it right now."

"You know, you're becoming a first rate investigator," I said, proud that she was learning what to look for.

"I wonder what a woman was doing in here," she said.

"I wonder if the woman was here before the blood got on the towel, or if the cologne got on the towel at the same time the blood did, or if it got on the towel after the blood. I would also like to know whose blood it is."

"Where did you say the matchbook was from?"

"The Whaler's Inn in Mystic."

"Where's that."

"I don't know. We'll have to look it up," I said as I put the matchbook in my pocket."

We continued to search the room until we were satisfied that we had found all we could. The two things that we never found were Jeff's laptop computer and his briefcase. There were no clothes in the closet or in the dresser. It appeared that the only things left behind that would give us any kind of a clue as to what happened was the matchbook and the bloody towel and sheets.

As soon as we left the room, the guard locked the door. We started back toward Sam's office. The guard fell in behind us. I wanted to talk to Monica about the matchbook, but with the guard right there, I decided that it would be best if I said nothing until later.

Sam was waiting for us when we returned to his office. He had fresh coffee and a snack on the table for us. It seemed to me that he was planning on us being there for a while. I also noticed that a large television and VCR had been set up in the corner of the room.

"Did you find anything?" he asked as he motioned for us to sit down at the table.

"No," I replied as I sat down. "The room was just as your housekeeper had said it would be. I found nothing that would help us find Jeff. However, the blood we found in the room tends to make me a little concerned for his safety.

"I'm sure it does. Maybe this will help. I have several surveillance tapes of Mr. Holcome playing Blackjack. Would you like to see them now?"

"Very much," I replied.

"This first one is from the Smoke Free Casino in Rainmaker Country. That's on the lower level," he said as he turned on the tape.

Monica and I settled in and watched the video in silence. We could make out Jeff playing Blackjack. He was at one of the lower limit tables. I figured that he might not want to lose too much money if his system didn't work. He seemed to be winning more than he was losing, which led me to believe that he may just have come up with a winning system, although it would be hard to prove from what we saw.

I noticed that there were several other people on the tape. There were at least three people just watching the game and four others at the table who were actually playing Blackjack. I took a little time to watch the other people on the tape. I wanted to be able to recognize them if I saw them again. No one seemed to be paying any attention to what Jeff was doing except for one man near the end of the table, but I couldn't be sure.

"Rather than have you here watching tapes for hours, I'm playing just the last twenty or so minutes of his three hour stay at the table. We can watch the rest of the tape if you like," Sam said as he shut off the tape and put in the next.

"That's fine. Let's see what this shows us first," I said.

"Mr. Holcome won just a little over a thousand dollars at that table before he moved on to the Rainmaker Casino. He moved to a table with higher betting limits. The Rainmaker Casino is directly above the Smoke Free Casino."

The next tape showed him playing Blackjack at a different table. Again, he was winning more hands than he was losing, just as he had in the other casino. He had built up a pretty good stack of chips in front of him that he seemed to be toying with as he played, just like he had before.

As I looked at the tape, I took note of those who were just standing around watching and of those who were playing at the same table. I noticed a woman who seemed to be just standing behind Jeff and watching him. I had seen her on the previous tape. The woman appeared to be in her mid-to-late thirties. She was wearing a red pantsuit outfit and a white pearl necklace. I wondered who the woman in red might be. She didn't seem to be with anyone, and she wasn't standing close enough to Jeff for me to believe that she was with him. But I had caught a glimpse of her off to the side on the previous tape.

I nudged Monica and leaned close to her. I whispered in her ear, "The woman in red."

As I watched, I also noticed a man who was playing Blackjack at the same table. It was the same man that I had seen on the previous tape as well. There were two people between the man and Jeff at the table, but with the curve in the table it made it easier for the man to keep an eye on what Jeff was doing.

"Are any of the people on these tapes your people, other than the dealer?" I asked Sam.

"No. Just the dealer. Why?"

"I just wondered. I just wanted to eliminate anybody I could as suspects right up front."

"That was his last twenty to thirty minutes at that table. Again, he spent three hours at that table," Sam said as he stopped the tape and took it out.

"By the way how much did he win at that table?" I asked.

"About two thousand dollars. He seems to know that game pretty well."

I looked over at Monica just as she looked over at me. I wondered if she was thinking the same thing that I was. I had to admire her ability to keep quiet and not say anything that would tip our hand in any way.

"This is the third tape that we found with him on it so far. We are still looking for others. As you will see, he is winning," Sam said as he slipped another videotape in the machine.

I turned my attention to the television screen again. Once again I saw Jeff playing the same game, Blackjack. He had a good size pile of chips on the table in front of him. He was playing with the top three or four chips just as he had done at the other tables. As I watched, I noticed that he again won more than he lost, but he seemed to be losing enough to make it look like he was just a good card player.

Once again I saw the women in the red pantsuit, only this time she was standing much closer to him. I noticed that Jeff looked back over his shoulder and said something to the woman. It must have been something she liked as she smiled, stepped up closer and put her hand on his shoulder.

The man was there too, only he was not playing cards this time. He was just standing back and watching. I noticed that he looked at the woman a couple of times, but his actions gave me no real clue as to whether he might know the woman in red.

I watched as Jeff got up, picked up his winnings and left the table. The woman in red walked away with him. Just before Jeff stepped out of the picture, he turned his head and said something to the woman. I couldn't make out what it was, but he looked pleased with himself.

"That's all we've found on him so far. I still have security looking for more tapes on him. Since he has been here two days, I'm sure we will find more tapes of him playing cards," Sam said.

"Good. We're going to be leaving to check out a lead. If you find anything else, keep it handy. We will be back late this afternoon or early tonight. If we find him, we will call you," I said.

"Okay. What about his room?" Sam asked.

"Do what you have to do. I don't think the police will find anything in the room that normally wouldn't be there, except for the blood. As far as I know, the police are not looking for Mr. Holcome."

"I think I'll have a good look around myself. If I find anything, I'll call in the police. If not, I'll let housekeeping get it back in use."

"That sounds good. If you find anything, you will let me know when I call you?" I asked as I stood up.

"Certainly. Keep in touch."

"I will," I replied as Monica stood up.

Monica and I left Sam's office and walked down the hall. We didn't say anything until we were well away from the security guard.

"Where to now? Mystic?" Monica asked.

"Yeah. We're going to find the Whaler's Inn."

CHAPTER SIX

We left the Knollwoods Resort and Casino and went out to the car. After getting in the car, Monica immediately found our map of the area and began looking for Mystic. I leaned over and looked at the map with her. It took us a few minutes to find where the town was located.

Mystic was an old whaling town where the Mystic River flowed out into the ocean. The town was now an historic community with a number of tourist attractions. The address on the matchbook indicated that we might find the Whaler's Inn very close to the center of the business district.

"Looks like we head for the coast," Monica said.

I started the car and began following Monica's directions. As we drove along, I began to wonder what was going on. With all the blood on the sheets in Jeff's room, I was wondering if we would even find him alive.

"Why do you think that Jeff went to Mystic? Do you think there might be a casino there where he could test his system some more?" Monica asked.

"I don't know why Jeff would go there. I'm not even sure that he did. And if he did, I'm not sure that it was his choice."

"You think he was taken there by force?"

"The matchbook was found in his room with several matches used, but we're not sure whether Jeff smokes or not. If Jeff doesn't smoke, that would indicate that whoever dropped it had already been at Whaler's Inn. If Jeff dropped it, that would mean he either had been to Whaler's Inn or he got the matches from someone who had."

"That's true. So why are we going there?"

"To find out if Jeff was ever there. Or to find out if the matchbook was dropped in his room by someone else. If someone else dropped the matchbook, maybe we will get lucky and find out who."

"Isn't this kind of a long shot?" Monica asked.

"Yes. A very long shot, but I don't want to leave one single stone unturned that might give us a clue as to where Jeff is and what he is doing."

Monica didn't say anything more. I could tell by the look on her face that she was wondering what our trip to Mystic might prove. I certainly had no idea what it might prove, but I had to follow up all the leads that we ran across no matter how thin they might be.

As I drove along, I kept an eye on what was behind us. I wanted to know if we were being followed. I noticed a white sedan that seemed to be staying just about the same distance behind us all the time. In order for me to be sure that it was following us, I changed lanes several times over the next several miles. I didn't want whoever it was to get suspicious and figure out that we were on to them. When I changed lanes, the car changed lanes, too.

"I think we've got a tail," I said as I changed lanes again.

"Which one?" Monica asked as she looked in her side mirror.

"That one. The white sedan that just changed lanes."

"I see it. I can't be sure, but it looks like there are two men in it."

"Yeah. I don't think I want to be followed just now."

"What are you going to do?"

"Ditch'um."

As casually as possible, I moved over one more lane from the right. I watched them as I moved in with the traffic, slowly pulling ahead of a group of slower cars on my right. When I saw that the white sedan was in the same lane that I was in, I slowly started to pass a tightly knit string of cars on my right. As they started to pass the same group of cars, I watched for an opening. As soon as I found an opening, I quickly turned and darted across the right two lanes of traffic and took an exit ramp off the Freeway. It was not the safest thing to do, but it caught them off guard. They were trapped in the wrong lane making it impossible for them to get off the Freeway on the same ramp that I took.

At the top of the exit ramp I stopped and watched them as they went on under the overpass. I turned left and crossed over the bridge in the hope that they would think we were going north. As soon as I was sure that they would not be able to see us, I turned into a driveway and turned around. I drove back over the bridge and headed back south. Instead of returning to the Freeway, I went on down the road turning onto a secondary road that would take us toward the town of Mystic.

"I'll bet they're mad as hell," Monica said with a grin.

"I'll bet they are, too. Now, let's see if we can find the Whaler's Inn."

Monica studied the map and gave me directions to downtown Mystic. I soon found myself in the middle of some pretty heavy tourist traffic. The streets were narrow and there were no empty parking spaces on the main street. It became clear that we were going to have to find some place to park the car and walk to the inn.

Monica spotted a parking space near a small park that ran along the edge of the river. We drove around to the space and parked the car. We got out of the car and started walking along the river back toward the main street.

The town looked like a step back in history of a hundred and fifty years ago or more. We walked along a wooden walkway that ran along the edge of the river.

There were a number of old pleasure boats, a few fishing boats, and a couple of sailing ships on the river. There was even a two-masted sailing ship slowly moving toward a drawbridge. I found it fascinating to watch the old drawbridge go up in order to let the sailing ship pass under it on its way to the sea.

When we reached the main street, we found ourselves on West Main. East Main was on the other side of the river, but we had to wait for the drawbridge to come back down before we could continue.

While we waited, I looked around. The storefronts had the look of the town when it was a whaling community. Although the stores did not contain ice cream shops, Tee-shirt shops, and gift stores when it was a whaling town, it still had the look of a whaling town during the late seventeen and early eighteen hundreds.

When the bridge finally came down, we walked on across. We soon found ourselves on East Main. It was not much of a walk to Whaler's Inn, maybe a couple of blocks.

Whaler's Inn wasn't a very big inn, but it was typical of those built in the late seventeen hundreds. It was two stories high with a large pillared porch across the front, and decorative woodwork accenting the colonial styling. There was a wrought iron fence that surrounded the small front yard. Inside the fence was a well-groomed lawn that sort of invited one to come in and stay for a while.

We walked through the wrought iron gate and up the steps to the porch. Once inside, we found the manager. She had her back toward us as she was dusting a large picture of a whaling ship that hung on the wall behind the check-in desk.

"Excuse me," I said to get her attention.

The woman turned and looked at us. A pleasant smile came over her face.

"Welcome to Whaler's Inn. How may I help you," the woman said with a heavy New England accent.

"I was wondering if you might have had a guest stay with you recently by the name of Holcome, Jeffrey Holcome?"

"No, I don't believe so," the woman replied after giving it a moment's thought.

"He was from Chicago. Does that help?"

"Oh, Yes. We did have a gentleman from Chicago, ah, something. Chicago Heights, that's it. He stayed with us until just the other day, but his name wasn't Jeffrey Holcome."

"What was his name?"

Tilman, ah, David Tilman. Yes, that's it, David Tilman. A very nice man."

"Could you tell me if he stayed here alone?"

"Oh my, no. He was here with his wife."

"Was she a fairly nice looking woman in her early-to-mid thirties with blond hair that was cut fairly short?"

"Why, yes. That's her. She was a very nice lady."

"Can you describe Mr. Tilman for me?"

"Well, let me see. He was medium height and weight, dark hair and a nice smile. Actually, he was rather handsome."

That description could have fit most of the men in this state. It not only fit the man we saw watching Jeff, but the description also fit Jeff. There was nothing specific in her description to narrow it down to Jeff, or the man on the tape, or anyone else for that matter.

"Can you tell me when they left?"

"I can't really say, but I'm sure that it was sometime early this morning. They didn't come down for breakfast. I can tell you this much, they were very careful and considerate people," she said with a smile of approval.

"What do you mean?"

"Why they even made their bed before they left. It wasn't necessary, of course, because we have to change the bedding anyway. But it was thoughtful of them, don't you think?"

"Yes, I'm sure it was. Thank you, thank you very much."

I took Monica by the arm and led her out of the inn. As soon as we got to the sidewalk, we began walking back toward our car. My mind was trying to put together what we had been told. I had to admit that I wasn't sure that we had learned much of anything.

My mind turned over and over the woman's comment about the bed. Why would anyone make the bed in a motel or inn when they were going to leave, especially in the morning?

"What's the matter, Nick?"

"I just thought of something."

"What?" Monica asked.

"The reason the bed was made was because they didn't sleep in it. They were not there last night. My guess is they stayed somewhere else."

"It seems clear to me that Jeff was never here," Monica said. "The matchbook was left in his room by Tilman or his wife."

"I agree with you that Jeff was not here. As for the Tilmans, I'm not so sure about them.

"What do you mean?"

"First of all, I'm not sure that the Tilmans are husband and wife. If they are, I wonder what their interest in Jeff was. Was it the disk, or was it the money he won at the Blackjack tables, or was it something else entirely?"

I could tell by the look on Monica's face that she could see that I might have a point. If they were after Jeff's winnings and got the disk too, then they may very well have gotten in way over their heads.

"I think it's time to get hold of Boyer again. We may have lost Jeff forever," I said.

The expression on Monica's face told me that she had not seriously considered that Jeff might already be dead. I had thought about it several times, but pushed it to the back of my mind. It was probably in the hope that if I didn't think of him as dead, we would find him alive.

We now knew that the woman we had seen in the tapes at Knollwoods had been here. The remaining question was who was the man in the tapes? My first thought was that it was David Tilman, that is if that was his real name. That was certainly a strong possibility. It was also a possibility that the man on the tape was not David Tilman. Our description of Tilman was too vague to make a positive identification of anyone. Plus, we had nothing solid that would connect Tilman to the woman on the tape. This had turned out to be a dead end, excuse the pun.

Just as I was about to say something to Monica, I noticed a white car coming down the street. I couldn't say for sure that it was the same car that I lost on the Freeway, but it sure looked like it. I grabbed Monica by the arm and literally dragged her into a little ice cream shop.

"What's the matter?" she said with surprise as she ducked around behind the door with me.

"I think that's the car that was following us," I said as I sort of hid behind a poster in the window and looked out.

Monica quickly moved behind me and looked over my shoulder.

"Is it them?" she asked as the car slowly went past the shop.

"Yeah. I think so."

"Any idea who they are?"

"Yeah, but nothing I can say for sure."

"What do you want to do?"

I looked around before I answered.

"I want to get an ice cream cone."

Monica looked at me as if I had lost my mind. But when I smiled, she could see the humor in it and we did just that. We each got an ice cream cone and sat down to enjoy them. It also gave me a few minutes to think about our next move.

"Nick, do you think Jeff is dead?" Monica asked in a whisper.

"I don't know, but I hope not," I said with a sigh.

"What's next?"

"We need to get to a telephone. I want to call Boyer and see if he has heard anything new."

"There's a phone right over there," Monica said as she pointed to a pay phone next to the door.

"Good. I'll call him from here. If they trace the call, they will end up here well after we're gone."

I left Monica at the table and went over to the phone. After dialing Boyer's cell phone number, I leaned against the wall and watched out the door for the car. Boyer answered his phone almost immediately.

"Boyer."

"This is McCord. Have you heard anything about Jeff?"

"Maybe."

"What do you mean 'maybe'?" I asked as I straightened up.

"The local police have found the car Jeff rented at the airport. We're on our way over there right now."

"Where is the car located?"

"It's behind a stone wall at the back of an old cemetery on highway 214 just west of Ledyard Center. Do you know where that is?"

"No, but we have a pretty good map of the area and I can find it."

"You better meet me there."

"Don't touch anything until I get there, understand?"

"Yes. I'll see to it that nothing is disturbed."

"We're on our way," I said, then hung up the phone.

I had no idea if Boyer would do as I asked. I wasn't even sure if he was running this show or not. With the local police involved, it was hard to say who was doing what.

"Come on. They found Jeff's car," I said as I approached Monica.

Monica stood up, reached out and took my hand. We hurried down the street and across the bridge toward where we had left the car. As soon as we got in, I started the car and pulled away from the curb.

"Look at the map and find me the shortest way to Ledyard Center. I want highway 214 going west out of Ledyard Center."

I took the first road that would take me north toward the interstate. It didn't take Monica long to find where I wanted to go and to start giving me directions.

We arrived at the small cemetery on highway 214 about two or three miles west of Ledyard Center. From the look of the grave markers, it was an old cemetery that probably dated back to the late seventeen hundreds. It was surrounded by a stone wall that had certainly seen better days.

As we pulled up, we could see two police cars and a black Chevy Tahoe parked off to the side. We could also see several men standing around a car that was partially hidden by the stone wall at the back of the cemetery.

I pulled around to the back, parked our car behind the Chevy Tahoe and got out. Monica followed me as I approached the men and the car. I noticed that Boyer was on the phone. When he saw me, he quickly hung up and walked toward me.

"This is the car Jeff rented at the airport. There's no one in it."

"Have you looked in the trunk?"

"No. You said not to touch it."

"Good. Let's take a look at it," I said as I started toward the car.

As I walked up to the car, the two police officers that had found the car just stood by and watched. Boyer moved up beside me.

"Are the keys in the car?" he asked the officer standing next to the car.

"No, sir," the officers replied.

"Have you got a pry bar? I need the trunk opened."

"I've got a tire iron," one officer suggested.

"That'll work. Open the trunk."

I stepped back away from the car and waited for the officer to get the tire iron. Monica moved up and stood behind me. I glanced over my shoulder at her. I could see by the expression on her face, that she was worried that we might find Jeff in the trunk.

"You might not want to see this," I said softly.

Monica looked at me, but didn't say anything. She just stood silently behind me.

The officer showed me the tire iron. When I nodded, he forced the end of the tire iron under the lip of the truck lid near the catch. It took him a couple of tries before the trunk lid finally popped open. I could hear Monica take in a deep breath when she saw the blanket lying in the trunk with a hand sticking out from under the edge of it.

Everyone stepped back and looked at me. My first thought was that we had found Jeff. I stepped toward the car while Monica remained where she was. I reached down, took hold of the corner of the blanket between two fingers and lifted it up. I expected this to be the end of our search for Jeff, but the man lying dead under the blanket was not Jeff. I wasn't sure who he was, but it was not Jeff.

Boyer walked up beside me and looked in the trunk. He then turned and looked at me.

"Do you know who this is?" he asked.

I did recognize him from the videotapes that Monica and I had seen at Knollwoods Resort and Casino. The only thing I lacked was a name to go with the face. It occurred to me that it might be David Tilman, but I could not be sure.

"No," I replied, not ready to let everything I knew out in the open, at least not yet.

I did a brief search of the body in an effort to see if I could find some form of identification. I found nothing on him that would identify him. I did find that a pocket had been torn off his tan coat. I also found a couple of poker chips from Knollwoods Resort and Casino. I quickly hid them in the palm of my hand before anyone could see them and slipped them into my pocket. In one pocket I found a half-empty pack of cigarettes. The one thing I didn't find was a book of matches or a lighter, but then I had a feeling that I already had the book of matches.

A closer look at the body showed that he had been shot in the head at very close range. A small caliber gun had been used and the shot had been very well placed. There was no doubt that he died quickly.

"Go over this car with a fine tooth comb. I want to know everything you can find out," I said as I turned and looked at Boyer.

"Okay. Where are you going to be?"

I hesitated to tell Boyer where I was going, but he had apparently kept his end of the bargain, so far. He had even gotten the local police to work with us. I wasn't sure how he had done that, but it gave me reason to trust him. Plus there was also the fact that I had no reason not to trust him.

"The Knollwoods Resort and Casino."

He gave me a funny look, but didn't say anything.

I turned around and looked at Monica. I could see by the look on her face that she was afraid that it was Jeff's body in the trunk of the car. I walked up to her and turned her around. I didn't want any one to hear what I had to say to her.

"It's not Jeff," I whispered in her ear as we started back toward our car.

"Who is it?"

"I don't know. He didn't have any identification on him. I'm sure that he was the man on the videotapes who was watching Jeff play Blackjack. He had two poker chips from Knollwoods in his pocket."

Monica looked up at me. I was sure that she was thinking the same thing I was. I wanted to know who the man was and why he had been following Jeff. I also wanted to know what his body was doing in Jeff's rental car. That fact alone made Jeff a prime suspect in his death.

"Let's go back to Knollwoods," I said.

"Nick!" Boyer called out to me.

"Yeah," I replied as I stopped and turned around to see what he wanted.

"We found this guy's wallet."

I glanced at Monica, then let go of her hand, and walked back to where Boyer was standing. He was holding a wallet.

"We found it under the blanket. It looked like it might have fallen out of his jacket when he was dumped in the trunk," Boyer said as he held the wallet out to me.

I took the wallet and opened it up. There was several hundred dollars in cash in it along with a driver's license. I took the driver's license out and looked at the picture. It was the dead man's driver's license. There was no doubt about that. The name on the license was that of David R. Tilman.

Although, it was interesting to find out what the dead man's name was, it was just as interesting to find out where he was from. The driver's license showed that Tilman was from Chicago Heights, Illinois.

I rummaged through the rest of the wallet. Besides the usual stuff a man carries in his wallet, I found a photo ID card from Games Unlimited. I looked at Boyer.

"Looks like one of your people. What was he doing here?" I asked Boyer as I held out the ID card for him to see.

There was a strange look on Boyer's face. He seemed surprised by my comment. It took him a moment or two before he looked at the ID card. When he finally looked at the ID card, it seemed to me that he was almost studying it. There was also the possibility that he was trying to think of what to say to me.

"I don't know this guy. I don't remember ever seeing him before," Boyer replied as he looked at the ID card. "He might be a corporate spy from another company. It wouldn't be the first time that one got inside the company."

“What do you suppose he was after?”

I watched Boyer’s face for any change in his expression, but saw none. Yet, I had this gut feeling that he knew more than he was letting on.

“That I don’t know. He could have been trying to find out if Jeff was about to introduce a new line of computer games. There’s a lot of competition in the field of computer games.”

“Enough to kill a man for?”

“Sure. One game can make or break a company in a matter of weeks.”

“Do you think he could have been after the disk that Jeff was to deliver?” I asked.

“I suppose it’s possible, but I doubt it. If he followed Jeff all the way out here, he was probably trying to get information on what new games he was working on, or what new games were coming out. Just a few weeks head start can make the difference between a successful year in sales or a total flop.

“There are a number of small companies out there that specialize in games. Some of their biggest games are card games for the computer. Jeff was one of the best in that field.”

I found his last comment very interesting. It might very well explain why Tilman was taking such interest in Jeff at the Blackjack tables.

“See what you can find out about this guy. I want as much information as you can get about him.”

“I’ll get right on it.”

“Call me at Knollwoods when you have something,” I said.

Boyer nodded that he would. I noticed that while we were talking, Boyer kept glancing over my shoulder. There was something behind me that was distracting him. I turned to see what it was that he found so interesting.

Parked on the other side of the cemetery was a white sedan. We could not see who was in it, but as soon as I started walking toward it, it started up and left. Whoever was in the car seemed to be in somewhat of a hurry to leave.

I turned and looked at Boyer. He seemed rather interested in the car, too. When he noticed that I was looking at him, he just shrugged his shoulders indicating that he had no idea who might be in the car.

As far as I was concerned, it was time to get out of here. I was sure that Monica had had enough of this place. I walked up to her and took her hand. We walked back to the car and got in.

The look on Monica's face told me that this was not something that she was likely to get used to, and I could understand. After all the years that I had dealt with murders while working for the Milwaukee Police Department, I still had never gotten used to seeing a dead body. It still bothered me, but I had learned to accept it as part of life.

"Are you all right?" I asked as I reached over and put my hand on her leg.

"Yes," she said with a sigh as she turned and looked at me.

"Lean back and take a couple of deep breaths," I suggested.

Monica did as I suggested, but I could see that it wasn't helping very much. I waited until she was ready.

"That was David Tilman. He was the same man on the videos that we saw watching Jeff at the Blackjack tables."

"Who do you think killed him?" Monica asked.

"I don't know," I said with a sigh.

"Do you think Jeff might have killed him?"

"It's possible. After all, Tilman was found in the car Jeff rented," I replied thoughtfully.

I've always been of the belief that anyone could kill someone if they were pushed hard enough. I was convinced that Jeff would certainly have motive enough if this guy was trying to steal his Blackjack computer game. Jeff would have wanted to protect that.

Anyone getting their hands on Jeff's system could not only win a lot of money before someone caught on, but could make the Blackjack tables a thing of the past. That is if it actually worked. Having people that were able to beat the odds at Blackjack would be reason enough for the Casinos around the country and around the world to want the system destroyed. That thought led me to believe that there may be others involved besides computer game companies.

"Well, we still haven't found Jeff. Where do you think he might be?" Monica said disturbing my thoughts.

"I don't know. He's due at the hotel in Hartford tomorrow for the conference. My guess is that he will not show up, but that is the next place he is scheduled to be. I think we should return to Knollwoods and see if he shows up there tonight. If he doesn't, then we go to Hartford tomorrow and hope that he turns up there."

"Okay," Monica agreed.

I leaned down to start the car. As I glanced out of the window, I noticed a car parked off the side of the road. It looked like it might have been the same car that left the cemetery in such a hurry. It was partly hidden behind some trees. I couldn't help but wonder who was in the car.

I waited until the road was clear, then backed out onto the highway. As I pulled away and headed east, the car pulled out onto the highway and followed us.

The more I thought about the car, the more I thought that it might be the General Dynamics security people on our tail. I thought about losing them, but then how would that make me look. It was time to let them follow me. I would rather know where they are, than not know.

"We have company again. I think I'll let them follow us this time. We are not very far from Knollwoods," I said.

Monica looked over at me as if I was crazy. I couldn't help but think that she might be right.

Monica and I arrived at Knollwoods Resort and Casino around three-thirty. We parked the car and walked to the Casino entrance. As we turned toward the doors, I glanced over my shoulder to see if we were still being followed. They were still there.

CHAPTER SEVEN

As we entered Knollwoods Resort and Casino, I glanced back over my shoulder one more time to see if the two men were still following us. This was the first time that I had ever seen these men. I had to wonder who they were and why they were following us. When Boyer saw them at the cemetery, he indicated that he didn't know who they were, either. If he didn't know, and I didn't know, than who were they? More importantly, who were they working for?

"It seems that there are a lot of people interested in us lately," I said with a smile as I slipped my arm around behind Monica and drew her close to my side.

"Really," she replied with a smile.

Monica was one smart lady. She seemed to know when to act as if we were having a good time and when to be serious.

"Yeah," I replied with a grin.

"What do you want to do?" she asked as she smiled up at me with a playful look on her face.

"I think I would like to know just who they are and what their interest in us is."

"How do you plan to do that?"

"I'm going to the restroom. Hopefully they will follow me. I want you to go directly to Sam Bradford's office and bring him back to the restroom."

"What if one of them follows me?"

"He wouldn't be stupid enough to try anything in here. Just lead him to Bradford's office and let Sam handle him."

"What if I can't find him?"

"Finds a security guard and bring him back here."

"Okay."

"I'll see you in a little while," I said, then leaned close to her and kissed her lightly.

I took my arm from behind her and stood for a moment outside the restroom entrance as I watched her walk away. As soon as she was well on her away, I turned and went into the restroom. I ignored the sign that said the restroom was closed for cleaning.

Once inside, I looked around. There was no one in the restroom. The custodian must have left to get something. I walked up in front of one of the urinals and acted as if I was using it. I watched out of the corner of my eye for the two men hoping that they would follow me into the restroom.

As luck would have it, only one of them came in. That indicated to me that the other one was following Monica. The one following me tried to act as if he wasn't paying any attention to me, but I knew better. He walked up to a urinal just a little ways from me. I finished, then turned as if to go to the sink to wash my hands. As I walked behind him, I quickly turned, stepped up behind him and stuck my finger in his back. I'm sure it was a little embarrassing for him when I poked him in the back.

"Zip it up," I ordered as I reached out and put one hand on his shoulder and held him at arms length.

"What's going on here?" he demanded, but zipped his pants.

"Over here," I instructed as I continued to hold him at arms length and guided him by the shoulder toward one of the stalls.

I shoved him through the door and into the stall, forcing him to straddle the stool. He practically fell over it.

"Put your hands on the wall. I suggest that you remain very quiet."

He leaned against the wall. Holding my finger in his back, I reached around and began patting him down. I quickly discovered that he was carrying a .38 caliber snub-nose pistol. I removed it from his shoulder holster.

"My, my. What do we need this for?"

"For people like you," he retorted angrily.

"Doesn't look like it's doing you much good, does it?"

"You caught me by surprise."

"In case you hadn't figured it out, that was the whole idea."

I held his gun on him while I lifted his wallet from his inside coat pocket, then I took a step back.

"I wouldn't move if I were you. Let's see who you are and why you're following me."

I opened his wallet. Inside was a Connecticut driver's license with a picture of the man I had leaning up against the wall. The name on the license was that of William A. Cooper. There were a few credit cards and a permit to carry a gun all with the same name. Other than some money, there was nothing else of interest.

"You mind telling me who you are?"

"You can read," he said defiantly.

"Don't be a smart ass," I said as I jabbed him in the ribs with the barrel his own gun.

"I'm a private investigator," he replied after taking a deep breath.

"Who are you working for?"

"That's confidential. That means it's none of your business," he said with a sarcastic tone in his voice.

"When someone follows me as close as you have, it becomes my business. Now, one last time, who you are working for?"

"I can't tell you," he insisted.

"I'm running out of time and I'm sure running out of patience. If you don't want me to turn you over to the house security and have him put you on ice for a while, you better start talking to me. Who do you work for and why are you following me?" I said as I jabbed him harder in the ribs with his gun to make my point very clear.

"Okay, okay," he said his face showing the pain from my jabs to his ribs. "I work for Games Unlimited. I was told that you were coming here to find Jeff Holcome. I figured that since you probably know Holcome better than I do, you might be able to lead me to him."

"It seems that there are a lot of people looking for Jeff. How did Games Unlimited know I was coming here?"

"My contact at Games Unlimited told me."

"Who's your contact?"

"I can't tell you that."

"You don't have a choice. On second thought, you don't have to tell me. Boyer is the Chief of Security for Games Unlimited. He would have to be the one who told you. He wanted you to keep an eye on me. Didn't he?"

"I don't know any Boyer. Besides, Boyer is not the Chief of Security at Games Unlimited."

"If Boyer is not the Chief of Security, then who is?"

Cooper let out a long sigh. It must have been clear to him that it would not take much to find out the name of the Chief of Security for Games Unlimited. A simple phone call would do it, so he might as well answer my question.

"Martin Springfelt."

Now that was a bit of news that I had not expected to hear. If Boyer was not the head of security, then who was he? My mind was going a mile a minute trying to figure out just what was going on here. My thoughts were disturbed by the sound of a voice coming from outside the restroom.

"Nick?"

"That you, Sam?"

"Yeah."

"Come on in."

I turned and looked as Sam Bradford came into the restroom with two guards.

"What's going on, Nick?"

"This guy has been following us. He says he's a private investigator working for Games Unlimited. I want him put on ice until we can pick up his friend and find out what's going on."

"We already have his friend. Monica pointed him out to us."

"Great."

"Take him to my office and hold him there till we get there. I need to talk to Nick for a minute," Sam told his security guards.

We stood in the restroom while the security guards cuffed and took Cooper to Sam's office. I wondered what it was that Sam had to say.

"Nick, I had a call from a man who identified himself as Kenneth Boyer. He said he was the head of security for Games Unlimited."

"I just found out that he might not be the head of security. What did he want?"

"He wanted to know if I could provide him with tapes of Jeff Holcome playing at the Blackjack tables."

"Really? What did you tell him?"

"I told him it would take me awhile to find them among all the security tapes, but that I would get on it. He seemed to accept that excuse and said that he would be calling me back."

"Good thinking. The man on the tapes that was watching Jeff so closely is dead. His name was David Tilman and his body was found in the trunk of Jeff's rental car."

"Do you think Jeff killed him?"

"It sure looks like he could have, but I don't know for sure who killed him. He was killed with a single shot to the head, almost too much like a professional job for Jeff to have done it, although it is possible. Tilman would have died almost instantly.

"If Jeff didn't kill him, then how did he get in the trunk of Jeff's car?"

"That I don't know."

"Any idea who might have killed him?"

"At the moment, no. Let's get up to your office. I'd like to find out what Cooper knows."

Sam nodded in agreement. I followed Sam out of the restroom, then walked with him to his office. When we arrived, I found Monica sitting on a chair in the outer office. Sam's secretary was sitting at her desk. The look on Monica's face told me that she was wondering what was going on.

"I was worried about you," Monica said as she stood up to greet me.

"I'm fine," I replied as I stopped, then reached out a hand to her while Sam went on into his office.

"Did you ever find out who David Tilman was?" Monica asked.

"No, not yet."

"Do you think that Sam could help us on that?"

"I sure hope so. Let's see what we can get out of this Cooper fella. Maybe he can shed some light on it."

Monica and I went into Sam's office. Sam was sitting behind his desk. Cooper was sitting on a chair with his partner sitting on a chair next to him. Standing near the door were two security guards that looked to be as big as mountains.

"I take it you would like to question these two," Sam said.

"Yes, I would. Cooper, just what was your job here?"

He looked at his partner, then at me. I think he was trying to decide just how much to tell me.

"I got a call from Games Unlimited."

"Martin Springfelt?"

"Yeah."

"Are you sure it was Martin Springfelt?"

"Yeah, I'm sure. We go back a long way. I've known Springfelt for fifteen years or more."

"Go on," I said waiting to hear what he had to say.

"Springfelt ask me to find Jeff Holcome and retrieve a couple of disks that he was supposed to have that rightfully belonged to Games Unlimited. It seems that he walked off with something he wasn't supposed to have. Martin wanted them back."

"What was on the disks?"

"I don't know. He never told me and I never asked."

"Do you know who David Tilman was?"

"Never heard of him."

Although he said he never heard of him, I noticed a slight twitch in his eye at the mention of Tilman's name. I got the impression that he did know him, or at least knew of him.

"You're lying to me."

"I don't know any David Tilman," Cooper insisted.

"Nick, could I have a word with you?" Sam asked as he stood up and started around to the front of his desk.

"Sure," I replied and stepped out of his office with him.

"Nick, I don't think we will get much out of him."

"I have to agree with you on that. He's not going to give us anything new."

"I can put him on ice, as you say, for a day or two, but that's about all."

"I need to find out more about this David Tilman and the lady in red," I said. "I would like to take another look at the tapes. Someone has to know who the woman in red is. Have you had any of your people look at the tapes?"

"A few. I have a few more from the hotel coming in to look at them when their shift is over. I'm hoping that someone will know her name, at least," Sam said hopefully.

"Good. I think we should let Cooper and his partner go. Do you have a couple of men you can trust to follow them?"

"Sure," Sam replied.

"Put a tail on them. I want to know where they go and who they talk to."

Sam nodded that he understood, then we returned to his office. I stood next to Monica and waited and watched as Sam walked around behind his desk.

"Escort these two out of here and make sure that they don't come back," Sam instructed the guards.

"You can't do that," Cooper protested.

"This is a casino on Indian land and I am head of security here. Would you like to make a little wager on whether or not I can keep you out of here?" Sam asked in a quiet, yet forceful voice.

He looked at Cooper for a second as if waiting for him to respond. When he didn't take up the challenge, Sam motioned for the guards to escort the men out. They left without further comment.

"Now what do we do, Nick?" Sam asked as soon as Cooper and his partner were gone.

"I would like you to call Games Unlimited and ask for the head of security. I want to know what his name is. If he says his name is Springfelt, you might ask him what he knows about Cooper."

"Will do. What are you going to do?"

"I think I will spend some time watching the action at some of your Blackjack tables."

"You can't cover all the tables from the floor, but you can see what is going on from our central monitoring rooms. I'll make arrangements for the two of you to get in."

"Thanks," I said.

I hadn't expected to get this much cooperation from the casino security, but I was glad to get it.

Monica and I waited in the outer office while Sam cleared it for us. I wasn't sure why Sam was so willing to help us, but I was sure that he didn't want a lot of bad publicity. It also crossed my mind that he might just be a little curious about Jeff's system. I could certainly understand his interest. If Jeff did have a system and Sam knew how it worked, he could keep a better watch over his Blackjack tables.

"Nick?"

"Yeah, honey."

"Do you think that Jeff is dead?"

"I don't know, but something tells me that he is alive."

"You seem so sure. Why?"

"I'm not all that sure myself, but if he was dead and anyone knew it, there wouldn't be so many people still looking for him. I'm sure the word would get out pretty fast."

"I guess you have a point, but maybe no one has found him yet."

"That's certainly possible, but think of this. Tilman was at the tables with him. Now he's dead. The woman who left with him has not turned up yet, and as far as we know, she was with Tilman last night. I think there is still hope that we will find Jeff alive."

Monica smiled slightly. I was sure that she could see my reasoning, but there was still that little bit of doubt in the back of her mind. I guess I couldn't blame her for that. I still had my doubts as well.

Just then the door opened and Sam came out of his office. He had a sad look on his face. My first thought was that he couldn't get us into the monitoring rooms, but that didn't seem to make any sense. After all, he was head of security. If the head a security couldn't get us in, no one could.

"I think you better come with me, Nick."

"What's wrong?"

"I think we may have found the woman in the red pantsuit," he said, then glanced over at Monica.

The sound of his voice and the way he said it made me wonder if the woman was already dead. If that was the case, the chances of finding Jeff alive seemed to be getting pretty slim.

I looked over at Monica. I was sure that she had seen enough dead bodies today and didn't need to see another.

"Monica, why don't you stay here," I suggested.

"No. I'm part of this team. I'm going with you."

I watched her as she stood up. She squared her shoulders and stepped up beside me. It was clear that she was putting on a pretty good show of strength. However, the way she took hold of my hand, holding it so tightly, was a good indication to me that she was frightened. Her courage made me feel proud of her.

We followed Sam through one of the casinos and out into one of the parking lots. As we came around a corner from behind some trees, we saw several tribal police cars with lights flashing. They seemed to be parked near the back of the parking lot.

When we got close to where the police cars were, we saw that an area just off the parking lot was being cordoned off to the public with bright yellow tape. It was an area where a narrow strip of grass ran between the curb of the parking lot and the woods.

As we approached, I noticed several tribal policemen back in among the trees. I could also see what looked like a body covered with a sheet. Sam walked up to the yellow tape and lifted it up. Monica and I ducked under it. A young officer started to tell us that we could not be there, but stopped suddenly when he saw Sam.

"Wait here," I suggested to Monica.

She looked toward the sheet that was on the ground in among the trees and then at me. She nodded that she would wait.

I turned and followed Sam to where the body lay. I knelt down and lifted a corner of the sheet. There on the ground lay the woman that I had seen on the tapes leaving the Blackjack table with Jeff, and she was very dead.

She had been a handsome woman in her early thirties, I would guess. I pulled the sheet off of her for a quick visual exam. My first impression was that she might have been sexually assaulted. But the more I looked at her and the way her clothes seemed to be arranged, I wasn't so sure. I slowly began to think that she had been put here to make it look like she had been assaulted.

Upon closer examination, it became clear to me that she had been shot at very close range. There were powder burns on the side of her head from a shot just behind her ear. It looked like it might have been from a small caliber gun. It was clear to me that she had been killed in almost the same manner as Tilman, a good indication that the same person or persons may have killed both of them.

I also noticed that she was missing one shoe. Where was the other? I stood up and began looking around, but didn't see the other shoe. A closer look at the ground next to the body showed no signs that she had been dragged here which could have explained the missing shoe. If she had been killed here, the shoe should have been close by and there should have been marks in the ground from her high heel shoes.

"Have everyone step back," I said to Sam, who was standing next to me.

"Everyone back," Sam ordered. "What are you looking for, Nick?"

I didn't answer him right away. I was looking for something, but I was not sure what it was. I stepped back and looked at the woman, and then I looked at the ground around her body. It became clear to me that the woman had been killed somewhere else and then her body had been carefully placed here.

"She wasn't killed here," I said as I glanced over at Sam. "She was laid out here to make it look like she had been assaulted and then killed here, but she wasn't."

Sam looked at the body, then around it. "I see what you mean."

“Cover her up, please,” I said as I looked back toward Monica.

Monica was standing close to the young officer who had greeted us when we ducked under the yellow tape. He was not paying any attention to her. He was watching us. I noticed Monica as she looked down at the ground in front of her. She then looked around before she bent down to pick something up out of the grass. I also noticed that she began looking around at the ground again as if she expected to find more of whatever it was she had discovered. She then bent down and picked up something else. This time she looked at me as she stood up.

I was curious as to what it was that she had found. She looked around to see if anyone was watching her, then slipped whatever it was she had found into her pocket and gave me a slight wink.

I got the message loud and clear. Whatever it was that she had found, she didn’t want anyone else to know about it, at least until she had a chance to show it to me.

“I’ve seen enough. Get some pictures of her and the surrounding area. You might want to be looking for her other shoe. It might give us some idea as to where she was killed,” I suggested.

“Okay. Anything else, Nick?”

“Yeah. See if you can find out who she is.”

“Right,” Sam replied.

I turned and walked back to Monica. Without saying a word, I took her by the arm and led her away from the area. We walked back toward the casino in silence.

As we entered the casino, Monica started to say something to me, but I cut her off. I had a feeling we were being watched and I wanted nothing overheard by someone nearby.

We walked through the building until we came to the Atrium Bar and Lounge. We were shown to a table in the corner of the room where I could see everyone who was nearby. As soon as we were seated, I looked at Monica.

"I saw you pick up something out there. What did you find?"

"I found a couple of pearls," she said as she reached in her pocket while looking around to see if anyone was watching.

Keeping her hands below the edge of the table, she held them out for me to see. I looked down at them. I had to wonder how they had gotten there. My first thought was that the woman had been wearing them, but I didn't remember seeing any of the pearls near the body. Monica had found them a good fifteen to twenty feet away from the body.

"They're real pearls," Monica said. "Very expensive."

"If someone had broken an expensive necklace out there, they certainly would have searched until all of them were found, you'd think," I said, thinking out loud.

"I know I would have. I think they were around the dead woman's neck. I remember seeing her on the tape. She was wearing a pearl necklace when she left with Jeff," Monica said as she looked over at me.

"I'll have Sam check the woman's neck to see if they were possibly ripped off her. If they were, it would have left a mark on her neck."

I was very pleased with Monica's observations.

"Just one question, why didn't you find any more pearls?"

"If the necklace had been cheap and had been ripped off her neck where I found these, I'm sure that there would have been more of them laying around. On the other hand, the most expensive pearl necklaces are tied between each pearl to prevent them from all coming off at once. The rest of the necklace would have remained intact. Since these are real pearls, my guess is that it was tied to prevent the loss of the pearls if broken."

"If they were tied, then that would mean that someone has the rest of the necklace."

"And that person might very well be the killer," Monica suggested.

"Right," I said as I wondered where the rest of the necklace might be.

"You think she was killed somewhere else, don't you?"

"Yes, I do."

"What do we do now?"

"We have some dinner, then go to the security monitoring room and watch the people play a little Blackjack," I suggested.

"Since we're here, why don't we eat here?" Monica suggested.

"Sounds okay to me."

Monica and I put our investigation aside for the moment and ordered dinner. It was a very relaxing time, one that allowed us to set things aside for a little while and enjoy our time together.

CHAPTER EIGHT

After we finished our dinner, we returned to Sam's office. At his instruction, we were escorted to the security monitoring room by one of his security people. As we entered the room, we could see several banks of television monitors that were being watched over by a number of security people. It was clear that they used the monitors to keep a surveillance of all the gambling areas and other public areas in all the different casinos within the complex.

The security guard led us toward a man who was looking over the shoulder of one of the security people. They were looking at a monitor with what appeared to be a great deal of interest. I wondered what might be going on.

As we approached the two, the man straightened up and looked toward us and smiled. Our escort introduced us to the room supervisor.

"This is Norman Winckler. He is the Monitor Room Shift Supervisor for the monitors covering the table games. He will show you around," our escort said, then turned and left the room.

"How do you do, Mr. Winckler. I'm Nick McCord and this is my partner, Monica Barnhart."

"Nice to meet you both. Please, call me Norm."

"I noticed that you were looking rather hard at that monitor. Is something going on?"

"No, not really. It seems we have a woman at one of the tables who has been losing a good deal of money. She claimed the dealer was crooked. We were just watching him a little closer to make sure that the dealer is honest."

"I see. Is he?"

"It looks that way," he said with a smile.

“Well, Sam told me you were coming. He said that you are primarily interested in what is going on at the table games, specifically the Blackjack tables. Is that correct?”

“Yes.”

“Well, you’ve come to the right place.”

“Good. The person we are looking for is most likely to be playing Blackjack.”

“Okay. Come with me, please,” he said then turned and started walking across the room.

We followed him past several banks of television monitors. There were several people sitting in front of them just watching what was going on. Some of the monitors showed people playing the slots, some playing roulette and others playing card games. There was also a bank of monitors that covered exits and entrances to the different casinos.

“These are the monitors that cover the Blackjack tables in the Grand Pequot Casino. They cover the Blackjack tables only.”

“Okay,” I replied.

“If you would like to pull up a chair, you can watch over Betty’s shoulder.”

“Hi, Betty. I’m Nick McCord,” I said.

“Hi,” she replied just glancing up at me then returning to watching the monitors.

“Betty will tell you what is going on. She will answer any questions you have.”

“What about the Blackjack tables in the Rainmaker Casino and the Casino I believe you call the Smoke Free Casino? They have table games as well, correct?”

“Yes, they do. Those are on other banks of monitors.”

“Would it be all right if Monica could sit in on one of those?”

“Certainly.”

“Nick, I know we’re looking for Jeff, but do you really expect to find him here after what has happened?”

"I don't know, but there's a chance that he is still here. But don't look just for Jeff. If he is still here, and if he is still playing Blackjack, he might have tried to change his appearance in some way."

"Do you think he would do that?"

"Regardless of what we have heard about him, I think Jeff might very well be a compulsive gambler. If he is not a compulsive gambler, he certainly is determined to test out his system. And I think he is smart. I got the impression that he has been working on this system of his for a very long time. I don't think he will be scared away from testing it very easily."

"Okay," Monica replied, but I got the impression that she didn't entirely agree with my thinking.

I watched as Monica was led away to a different set of monitors. I couldn't blame her for not being totally convinced that I was right. I wasn't even totally convinced myself.

After she had disappeared around a corner, I pulled up a chair and sat down next to Betty. I looked up at the monitors and wondered how anyone could keep track of what was going on.

"As you can see, Mr. McCord, we can see what the dealer is doing and what all the players at the table are doing."

"What is it you watch for?"

"We watch for a number of things. We watch for players that cheat. Slipping cards on or off the table. Players that are winning or losing too much throws up a red flag. We watch them closely."

"Losing too much?"

"Oh yes. Those are the players that are most likely to become a problem, you know, cause trouble. They sometimes try to cheat, or they blame the dealer for cheating, or they get angry and become a threat to others around the table. We like to head off trouble before it gets out of hand."

"I see."

"We also watch winners. There is always the possibility that they are working with the dealer. Even though we screen our dealers, occasionally we get one that will partner up with a player and try to cheat so the player wins a lot of money. They usually split up the winnings later."

"That makes sense."

"The game is in the house's favor anyway. We are just trying to let the game play out with its normal odds."

"I guess that makes sense."

"We also watch for winners as they leave the tables. We don't want any of them getting robbed while they are here by someone who has been watching them. If we have a big winner, we have a security guard keep an eye on him, usually without the customer knowing it. It's good for business if the customers feel safe."

"It sounds like you are trying to keep the games on the up and up."

"We are trying to do just that. Our reputation depends on it. If we don't run a clean business, we would lose business. We would also have the gaming commission on our backs, and no one wants that."

"I would think not."

"What is it you are looking for?" Betty asked.

"We are looking for someone who is winning more than he is losing. It is a man, but if he has changed his appearance, he could look like anyone."

"Okay, I'll keep an eye out for a winner."

"Good, but remember he loses sometimes. You might try to look for someone who thinks he has a system."

"That could be almost anyone. It seems that everyone has a system now days. The problem for them is that those so called "systems" just don't work."

"I wouldn't be too sure that this one doesn't work," I said as I looked up at one of the screens.

I took my time watching each screen for a few minutes at a time. The players seemed to come and go. That thought gave me an idea.

"One other thing, you might keep an eye out for someone who stays at the same table for a long period of time. Say, for two or three hours. The man we're looking for stayed at the same table for three hours, then moved to a different casino."

"That might help," Betty replied as she continued to watch the monitors.

As I watched the screens in front of me, I began to wonder just what Jeff was up to. He was supposed to deliver a disk to General Dynamics, but according to Boyer he never delivered it.

He was supposed to go to Hartford to a computer games conference, but he took a three-day side trip here to play Blackjack and didn't tell his wife. The body of a man who had been watching him play Blackjack was found in the trunk of his rented car, and the body of a woman who had left the Blackjack table with him was found dead just outside the casino. Nothing seemed to make sense.

My mind tried to search for information as to what he was doing. The question of whether he was alive or not was still haunting me. I had nothing to prove that he was alive, but on the other hand I had nothing to prove that he was dead. If he was alive, where was he going to show up next?

Suddenly, something on one of the screens caught my attention. I found myself staring at the screen and at an individual who was playing Blackjack. It had just registered in my head that this man was winning fairly regularly. He would win three or four hands, then lose one or two. He was winning more than he was losing.

I glanced over at Betty and noticed that her attention seemed to be on the same screen that I was watching. I wondered if she had taken notice of the man, too.

"I think we might have something for you," she said as she pointed at the same monitor that I was watching.

"Yeah, I see him."

"Do you think that's the man you're looking for?"

I moved up a little closer to the screen in the hope of getting a better look at him. It didn't look like Jeff, yet there was something about him that seemed familiar.

"How tall do you think he is?" I asked.

"He's about five-eleven, maybe six foot tall," Betty replied.

"He's about the right height, but he looks heavier than the man we're looking for. His hair isn't right, either," I said, still unsure if it was him.

"His clothes could make him look heavier, and he could be wearing a wig of some kind or he could have changed his hair style and color," Betty suggested.

I knew she was right, but I still couldn't be sure. I felt I had to be sure before I took any action. If I had him picked up by security and he was not the right man, the commotion could spook Jeff into running. If he ran, I might have a very hard time finding him again.

"How long has he been playing at that table?"

"Only about thirty minutes."

"He doesn't look like he has very much money, does it?"

"Not very much. He's won about half of what he has in front of him since he started," Betty said as she continued to watch him.

I continued to watch the man as he played. I noticed that he began to lose more than he was winning. It looked as if the tables had turned against him.

"If this guy has a system, it's how to lose in a hurry," Betty commented. "Did you see that? He just made a big bet and lost it all."

I watched as the man tipped his head back and looked up in disgust. It was then that I got a better look at the man's face. It was easy to see that he was not Jeff.

"That's not him," I said, a little disappointed.

I returned to looking at the other monitors, going from one to the other. I watched but nothing seemed to click. I was beginning to think that we were not going to find Jeff, at least not tonight.

"Nick."

I turned to see Monica standing next to Norman Winckler. She motioned for me to come over to where she was. I excused myself and immediately got up and went over to see what she had found.

"What do you have?" I said as I stepped closer to Monica.

"Right there," she said as she pointed at one of the monitors.

I looked at the monitor, but all I saw were three women playing Blackjack. One woman looked to be in her mid-sixties. She seemed to be having a bit of luck at this table. Another woman looked like a younger version of the older one, probably her daughter.

"Look at that woman," Monica said as she pointed at the third women. "Notice anything different about her?"

"No," I said as I studied the woman.

"That's not a woman," Monica said with a grin.

I looked at Monica, then back at the monitor. I watched the woman and her moves. There was something about her that didn't set well with me, but I was having a hard time figuring out what it could be. It then hit me.

"I believe you're right," I said. "What do you think, Norman?"

"She might be right," he said. "I guess it takes all kinds."

"Yeah," I replied as I began to take more interest in the woman.

The more I watched the woman, the more I realized that there was something different about her, other than the fact that she was much taller than the other two women at the table. There was something about her movements. They seemed to lack the softness and smoothness of the movements of most women. And, there was something vaguely familiar about her.

I tried to look at her with an open mind in an effort to figure out what it was that I couldn't see that I should be able to see. I tried looking at what she was doing. She was playing Blackjack, but so were the other two women. It was clear that she was winning more hands than she was losing.

Then it came to me with the subtlety of a hit in the head. My eyes immediately went to the pile of chips stacked in front of the woman. I noticed that they were stacked in a certain order and I found myself staring at them.

"That's Jeff," I blurted out.

"What?" Monica said with surprise.

"I'd be willing to bet that's Jeff. Look at the chips. They're stacked just like he had them stacked in the videos we saw of him yesterday. And notice how he plays with just the top three or four chips on the second pile? It's like a signature. By playing with the chips like that, he gives himself away and doesn't even realize he is doing it."

"Are you sure?" Norman asked.

"Yes. Yes I'm sure."

Monica leaned just a little closer to the monitor. I could tell that she was studying the woman's movement.

"My God, you might be right. I think it is Jeff," she said with a note of surprise.

"Where is he playing?" I asked Norman as I turned to look at him.

"He would be in the Rainmaker Casino. Ah, table six."

"How long has he been there?"

"Just about three hours," the person monitoring the screen said after looking up at the clock above the monitors.

"If that is Jeff, he'll be leaving soon if he follows his pattern. How long will it take us to get there?"

"Five or six minutes, if we're lucky," Norman answered.

I didn't wait for any further conversation. I turned and headed for the door with Norman hot on my heels.

As I stepped out of the monitoring room, I turned toward Norman.

"Which way?" I asked figuring that he would know the quickest way to get to the Rainmaker Casino.

"Follow me," he said as he took off down a long narrow hallway.

I followed him down the hallway, then down a couple of flights of stairs and out into the hallway that was used by the public. The place was busy and it was difficult for us to move very fast through the crowd of people that were milling around without pushing people out of the way.

As we moved toward the Rainmaker Casino, I saw Norman reach to his hip and grab his two-way radio. I could not hear what he was saying, but I was sure that he was trying to get a couple of his security people over to the blackjack table to find the woman, or at least watch the exits and prevent the woman from leaving.

When we got to the Rainmaker Casino, I noticed several security people at the entrance. There were always one or two, but now there were six and they all seemed to be looking for someone. I could see it would be difficult for anyone to slip out of the casino without someone seeing them.

"Have you seen the woman?" Norman asked one of the security people at the entrance.

"No, sir. She hasn't come out this way."

I stood by and listened as Norman checked with his security people at each of the entrances. All of them reported that the woman he had described to them had not left the casino floor.

"Looks like she is still in the casino."

"I hope so," I replied. "Where's table six?"

"This way."

I followed Norman across the floor of the casino toward table six. The place was crowded and noisy from the bells and whistles of the slot machines. I tried to see if I could find anyone that even came close to fitting the description of the woman that we had seen on the monitor, but with no luck.

"Secure one, Secure one," I heard Norman's two-way radio blurt out.

Norman reached for his two-way and replied, "Secure one, go ahead."

"The woman at table six gathered her chips and left the table just as you went out the door. It looked as if she was headed to the Cashier Windows."

"Thanks."

Norman made a sudden turn and headed toward the Cashier Windows. I was right behind him. When we arrived, there were only a couple of people standing around waiting to cash in their chips. None of them came close to matching the description of the woman we were looking for.

We stopped and looked around. I couldn't see anyone in the crowd that looked like the woman we had seen. In a way, I had been sure that it had been Jeff, but now I wasn't so sure.

"I think we lost her," Norman said.

I could hear the disappointment in his voice.

"Yeah, but do you have this placed pretty well sealed off?" I asked.

"I hope so."

Norman once again got on his two-way radio and talked to security guards at each exit from the Rainmaker Casino. Each security guard reported that no one answering the description that we had given had left the casino. That meant that if it was Jeff, he was either still in the casino, or he had changed his appearance in some way and slipped out.

Norman ordered an aisle by aisle, area by area search of the entire casino, including the restrooms. While I waited for some news, I turned around and asked one of the cashiers if she had seen anyone cashing a large number of chips in the last ten or fifteen minutes. She said that no one had cashed in chips for more than two or three hundred dollars during that time frame. I was sure that the chips stacked in front of the woman amounted to much more than two or three hundred dollars.

"It looks like our woman has disappeared with her chips," Norman said.

"Looks like it," I said, disappointed that we were unable to find the woman. "How do you think she got out?"

"I don't know. She might have decided not to cash in her chips. If she did that, she could have gotten out of here before we had a chance to get all the exits sealed off."

"I guess that's possible. On the other hand, if it was Jeff, he may have found a place to change out of his dress and walked out without anyone noticing."

"I guess that's possible, too," Norman agreed.

"My guess is that he knows he is being watched by your security people. That's the reason for dressing up like a woman."

"One good thing is that he can't use those chips anywhere but here. He will have to cash them in sooner or later if he wants the money for them," Norman said.

"Yeah. That means that he either plans to return to do some more gambling, or he plans to cash them in later when he thinks things have cooled down a little. If he waits 'til later to cash them, we could have a very long wait," I added.

"We'll be watching for him," Norman said with a tone of confidence.

"I'm sure, but what will he look like next time he comes in here? There's always the possibility that he will get someone else to cash in his chips for him. Maybe he will only cash in part of them at a time to avoid suspicion."

Norman just looked at me. I was sure that he could see my point. The only thing we could do now was to wait for Jeff's next move.

After all of Norman's security people had made a complete sweep of the casino and reported that they were unable to find anyone that fit the description given them, I let out a long sigh. I was disappointed as I really felt we had been very close to finding Jeff.

Norman and I left the Rainmaker Casino and returned to the Monitoring room. When we arrived, Monica was waiting for me. I could see by the look on her face that she was just as disappointed as I was.

"Didn't find him?"

"No. If it was him, he slipped out."

"What do we do now?"

"We could start monitoring the other casinos, but I don't think it will do any good tonight. If that was Jeff, my guess is that he knows someone is looking for him and he won't be back for a while. He will keep a low profile for a day or two. The one thing we do know is that he will return here. He has too much money in chips to just leave it."

"Maybe not," Monica said.

"He had at least a couple thousand dollars in chips on the table when he left," I said, wondering what she was getting at.

"Yes, he did. But if he has the winning system that he thinks he has, he could leave the chips somewhere and move on to another casino in a different city where he could win more money. He could always return here months from now and cash in his chips. There is nothing that says he can't just hang onto the chips for months."

Monica had a very good point. It sure put a hole in my balloon. I had to give this some thought. Although I agreed with Monica's assessment of the situation, I had the feeling that Jeff would stay in the area a little longer. There was still the matter of the disk. We had no idea what had happened to it.

"I think he will stay around here. As far as we know, he still has the disk he was to deliver to General Dynamics," I said as I took Monica by the hand.

We walked out of the monitoring room and started down the long narrow hallway. I could see that Monica was thinking about what I had said. Suddenly, she stopped and looked up at me. I could tell that she had something on her mind.

"What?"

"I just had a thought," she said looking as if she hadn't completely put her thought together, yet.

"What is it?"

"How do we know that Jeff didn't deliver the disk to General Dynamics?"

"What are you saying?"

"I'm saying that we have been taking Boyer's word for it that Jeff didn't deliver the disk. Who is Boyer? He told us that he was working for Games Unlimited, but we just found out that he doesn't, or at least there's a very good chance that he isn't who he said he was."

She was right. With all that had happened during the past few hours, and my efforts to find Jeff, I had put any thoughts of Boyer in the back of my mind. It was then that I remembered that I had asked Sam Bradford if he would check on Boyer in an effort to verify what Cooper had told us. I began to wonder if Sam had had time to follow up on it with all that had happened tonight.

"We need to check with Sam and see if he found out anything about Boyer," I said.

"I think it would be a good idea if we find out who the Chief of Security is at General Dynamics and ask him if he got the disk from Jeff," Monica said.

"I think you're right," I agreed as I looked at my watch.

"It's a little late to call General Dynamics now," Monica said as she glanced at her watch. "All we would get is some guard that probably wouldn't know anything about it.

"You're probably right. I'm sure we could get someone in security, but I would prefer to talk to the head man."

"Do you think that Sam would be in? He might have found out who the security chief of General Dynamics is."

"He's had a pretty busy evening. I kind of doubt it. My guess is he is tied up with the police over the dead body found on the grounds of his casino, or that he has gone home for the night after a very disturbing day."

"Maybe we should call it a night, too," Monica suggested.

"You're probably right."

I took Monica by the hand and we walked out into one of the main hallways of the casino. We moved among the people on our way to the elevator that would take us to the floor that our room was located on.

I was not really paying much attention to those around us. I had already come to the conclusion that there was nothing more we could do tonight. My attention was on the woman whose hand I was holding.

I didn't notice the man approaching us at first. I saw him, but he didn't register in my mind until I actually made eye contact with him. It was Sam and he looked as if he might have something important to say.

"Nick," he called out as he raised his hand to get my attention.

I raised my free hand to let him know that I had seen him. He motioned for us to turn. I looked off to the side and noticed a large window with a bench in front of it. I guided Monica over to the bench where Sam joined us.

"I thought you would have gone home by now. What's up?" I asked.

"It has been a busy day, but that's the way it goes around here. I wanted to let you know that I got hold of the head of security at Games Unlimited. It turns out that Cooper was right. His name is Martin Springfelt, and he personally hired Cooper to find Jeff Holcome."

"Was he able to tell you anything about Boyer?"

"No, but he said he would check around and see what he could find out about him."

"Good."

"What about the woman? Have they found out who she is?" Monica asked.

"No, not yet. But I'm working on it."

"I guess we're going to call it a night. But I would like you to do something for me."

"What's that?" Sam asked.

"I would like you to find out the name of the head of security at General Dynamics."

"That should be no problem. I'll get it for you first thing in the morning."

"Great. We'll see you in the morning."

"But not too early," Monica added.

"I don't think I'll be in very early myself. How about meeting here for an early lunch?" Sam suggested.

"Sounds good," I replied. "About ten?"

"Good. See you tomorrow," Sam said, then turned and walked away.

It wasn't long before Monica and I were back in our room. It had been a long day with a lot of things happening. We were both very tired. We wasted no time in climbing into bed and cuddling up against each other. In a short time, we were both sound asleep.

CHAPTER NINE

When morning came, Monica was lying beside me. I could feel the warmth of her body against my back and her breath on the back of my neck as she cuddled up against me. I could also feel her arm lying over me as she gently ran her fingers through the hair on my chest. Starting off the morning with this gorgeous woman holding me was my idea of the perfect way to start the day.

"I'll give you twenty minutes to quit that," I whispered.

"And if I don't?" she asked with a smile in her voice.

"I'll give you another twenty minutes."

"I love you," she whispered softly in my ear.

"I love you, too."

"Are you ready to get up?"

"No. I want you to spend a little time with me," she said softly, her voice so sexy that I could not refuse her request.

Spending time with her was certainly no problem for me. I liked being with her. I rolled over so that I was facing her and took her in my arms and held her tight. As we kissed, I gently rolled her up over me. The feel of her warm naked body stretched out over me removed all thoughts from my mind of anything except for those thoughts of her and how much she meant to me.

I slowly slid my hands up and down the smooth flowing lines of her back. Her skin felt soft and sleek. Her body was not only a pleasure to touch, it was exciting to touch. The fact that she seemed to like having me touch her certainly didn't hurt matters any, either.

She lifted up a little and looked down at me as I slid my hands over her shapely body. She smiled and her eyes sparkled in the morning light that slipped in around the edges of the curtains. She sort of reminded me of a kitten that was being petted. I think I could even hear her purr a little.

"I like the way you touch me," she whispered as I looked into her exquisite cobalt blue eyes.

"I like touching you," I replied as I slid my hands down over the sensual curves of her shapely butt.

She smiled then laid back down over me again. Our lips met in another warm, passionate kiss. The feel of her firm breasts pressing against my chest only deepened the passion of our kiss. This was a time for us to enjoy each other. I wanted nothing to disturb this moment, but it was not to be.

Suddenly, our private little world was invaded by the rude and harsh ringing of the telephone. Needless to say, I didn't want to be interrupted, especially at this time. But with all that had been going on over the past few days, I didn't feel that I could ignore the phone.

Monica lifted herself up and looked down at me. The look on her face told me that she didn't want me to answer the phone, either. Yet, at the same time, I think she must have realized that it might be important. Reluctantly she rolled off me so that I could reach the phone on the bedside stand.

I rolled over, reached out and picked up the phone. I could feel Monica roll up against my back as I put the receiver to my ear.

"Hello?"

"Nick, this is Sam. I hope I'm not disturbing you."

I knew Monica could hear him. She gave me a gentle squeeze indicating to me that she had been disturbed by his call. I had to agree with her, but I wasn't going to say anything to Sam about it.

"No. What is it?"

"I have a couple of things to tell you. First of all, one of my people found a shoe that matches the one found on the dead woman. It was found in one of the dumpsters back of the hotel."

"Well, I think that answers one of our questions. She was probably killed here in the hotel."

"You think she might have been killed in Jeff's room?"

"Yeah. That would be my guess."

"That sure would account for the blood on the sheets," Sam agreed. "But didn't you say that she was seen in Mystic that night."

"She was supposed to have stayed at Whaler's Inn in Mystic that night, but we don't really know that she did. From what the manager at the Inn said, I don't think they ever actually stayed there. She told us that they made the bed in the morning and that she did not see them leave," I explained.

"That could mean that they never spent the night there. They could have checked in, come back here where they were killed, and never got back to Mystic," Sam said as if he was thinking out loud.

"That's a very strong possibility. What was the other thing you wanted to tell me?" I asked.

"Oh. You know that I called Games Unlimited in Chicago and found out that Martin Springfelt is the head of security at Games Unlimited?"

"Yes. What about it?"

"Well, he called me this morning. He said that he would get in touch with Cooper and tell him that he is to cooperate with you in any way he can."

"Well, at least that's one person following us that I don't have to worry about. Was he able to shed any light on Boyer?"

"No. He says he still doesn't know who Boyer is, but that he would keep looking into it. He said that he would get back to me if he finds out anything."

"That's something at least."

"Yeah. I thought you would like to know."

"Did you find out who the head of security is at General Dynamics?"

"Not yet," he replied. "I hope to have that for you when we meet for an early lunch. We are still meeting for lunch?"

"Yeah, sure. Where?"

"Let's meet at the Veranda Café on the Mezzanine level in the Grand Tower," Sam suggested. "I'm buying."

"That makes it hard to refuse. We'll see you there in a little while."

"Great."

I leaned over and hung up the phone. I turned my head and looked over my shoulder at Monica. She leaned toward me and kissed me. The feel of her body against my back and the warmth of her kiss made me want to call Sam back and tell him that we would rather have a late lunch.

"We better get up," Monica said with a slight tone of disappointment in her voice.

"Yeah," I agreed reluctantly.

Monica let go of me and rolled over on her back. I swung my legs over the side of the bed. As I sat on the edge of the bed, I looked back over my shoulder at her. She was so beautiful lying there. Her long blond hair was fanned out over the pillow, her cobalt blue eyes looking at me and her naked body stretched out on the covers.

"God, you're beautiful," I said as I let my eyes look her over.

She smiled and reached out a hand to me. I took hold of her hand and raised it to my mouth. I lightly kissed her hand and smiled at her.

"As much as I would like to forget about this early lunch with Sam, I think we need to go. He might have information that we can use."

"I agree," she replied, but her agreement lacked any kind of enthusiasm.

I let go of her hand and stood up. I went into the bathroom and turned on the shower. As soon as the water was warm, I stepped in.

I stood in the shower and let the water run over me. It felt good and cleared my head. I began to go over in my mind all that had happened over the past couple of days. Although I was wondering about where Jeff might be, the biggest question that came to mind was what was Jeff doing? What was on Jeff's mind? And more importantly, had he killed the woman and Tilman in his room. That would certainly explain the bloody sheets and towels.

Of course, I had no answers - just questions. There had to be something that I was missing, something that I hadn't thought of. All I could hope for was to get one question answered at a time. The one that Monica had brought to my attention last night was the one that I wanted answered first. Had the disk been delivered to General Dynamics?

Everything up to now had indicated that the disk had not been delivered, but that was what we had been told by Boyer. We had no first hand information to confirm it one way or the other. That question alone could clear up a lot of other questions. It could also create a lot more questions.

I got out of the shower and dried off. When I entered the bedroom, I saw Monica on the phone.

"He's here now. Would you like to speak to him?" I heard her ask.

Monica looked at me, then held out the phone.

As I took the phone, Monica whispered, "It's Boyer."

I wasn't sure I wanted to talk to him just yet. I still didn't know who he was working for, or what part he played in all this. The one thing I did know about him was that he was not who he had said he was.

"Hello, Boyer."

"Hello. I understand that you were followed back to the casino yesterday. Was it that car we saw at the cemetery?"

"I think so."

"Did you find out who was following you?"

"No."

"I also heard that a woman was found dead in the casino parking lot. You know anything about that?"

"No," I replied, not wanting to let anything out that might give him an edge.

"You must know something about it. You and your lady friend were on the scene with the head of security from the casino. You were there a good twenty minutes or more."

Well that sure answered one question. There was no doubt in my mind that Boyer was still having us followed, but then I had expected that he would so it was no big surprise. Since I found out that he didn't work for Games Unlimited, I was sure that his interest in Jeff was for his own personal gain or whomever he was working for.

"We may have been on the scene, but we still don't know who she is or why she was killed."

"Is Mr. Bradford helping you?"

"We sure have a lot of questions this morning," I said, ignoring his last question.

"Well, I don't think you're sharing information with me, Mr. McCord. After all, you are working for me. We have an agreement, or did you forget about that?"

"I didn't forget anything. Besides, I'm not working for you, Boyer. I'm working for Games Unlimited," I reminded him.

"That may be true, but I'm your contact for them. Therefore, you answer to me."

There was something about the sound of his voice that bothered me. It was soft, almost as if he were trying to convince me of something that I wasn't buying into. Yet, behind his words and in the sound of his voice there was a quiet threat. I've never liked being threatened and I don't take kindly to threats, not from him or anyone else.

"Let's get one thing straight, Boyer. There are only two people I answer to, Miss Barnhart and myself. I will give you information when I'm convinced that the information I have is good, solid information, and I can prove it to be accurate.

"Speaking of agreements, I haven't seen one dime toward our expenses from you or Games Unlimited. I think it would go a long way in improving our business relationship if you started paying for what we agreed on."

"I'm sure that you will receive what is coming to you when this is over," he said.

It was clear to me what he meant, even if I was supposed to take it in a different light. His last comment was well covered, but it was a threat just the same. I had no interest in talking to him any longer. I needed to know more about him before I was going to give him anything more.

"I have to go. I have a couple of things that I need to follow up on," I said.

"What do you think you found?"

"I'll let you know later when I know something," I replied then hung up the phone before he could respond.

I was sure that Boyer was not happy with me for hanging up on him. I had told him nothing and he knew it. From now on I would have to be very alert and watch my back. There was no doubt that Boyer would have someone on my tail all the time.

"Do you think he suspects that we know he is not the head of security at Games Unlimited?" Monica asked, her question interrupting my thoughts.

"I don't know. If he doesn't suspect something is wrong, then he's not very smart."

"If he does, I think he will try to keep very close tabs on us," Monica added.

I couldn't have agreed with her more, but I couldn't worry about him right now. I needed to meet with Sam and find out what he found out about the woman in the red suit, and if he found out the name of the head of security at General Dynamics.

Monica and I finished getting ready for our luncheon date with Sam Bradford. As soon as we were ready, we left our room and walked down the long hall to the elevator. I watched to see if we were being followed by anyone, but I saw no one in the hall, not even a maid or a maid's cart.

We took the elevator down to the Mezzanine Level. As we stepped off the elevator, I noticed a man in the usual green blazer of the security people. As we made eye contact, he nodded slightly to acknowledge that he had seen me. As I walked past him, he said nothing. He simply stood at his post watching the people who were milling around.

As we entered the Veranda Café, I saw Sam standing next to a tall man wearing the customary green blazer. It looked as if Sam was giving the man instructions. I noticed the man nod as an indication that he understood what he had been told. He then turned and left the café.

Sam saw us and motioned for us to come and join him. I slipped my hand behind Monica and guided her across the room toward Sam. When we got close, Sam pointed to a table where we sat down with him. There was a young waitress standing next to the table. After we were seated, she took our order, then left us alone.

"Good morning," Sam said. "I hope you had a pleasant night."

"Yes, we did," Monica replied with a smile.

"Have you found out who the woman was?" I asked wanting to get right down to business.

"I got a call from a friend of mine on the police force. He said her name was Barbara Whitman."

I looked at Monica, then back at Sam. The name meant nothing to me. I could not recall ever having heard the name before.

"She was apparently from Chicago. She arrived on the same plane that Mr. Holcome arrived on."

That piece of information caught my attention. I began to wonder if Jeff knew her. If he did, that could mean a lot of things, or it could mean nothing at all.

"Is there any indication that they might have known each other before arriving here?" I asked.

"Not that we know of. At least not yet. From what we have been able to find out so far, there is no connection between them prior to their meeting here," Sam said. "Even the video tapes from the casinos showing them at the same table seem to indicate that they met here."

"Unless it was meant to look that way," Monica added.

Just then our meals arrived. I sat back and thought about the possibilities as I could envision them while the waitress set our plates on the table. I was reasonably sure that Jeff knew that he would be watched. He had to know that much, and he proved it by dressing as a woman when he played Blackjack last night.

"So you think she picked him up here?" Monica asked.

"We think so, but there is always the possibility that it was a planned pickup," Sam admitted. "You know, staged for the benefit of whoever was watching, namely the security cameras."

"Didn't you say they were on the same plane?" Monica asked.

"Yes," Sam replied.

"Then it's possible they met on the plane," Monica said.

"Let's say for the sack of argument that she met him here for the first time. She picked him up rather quickly, don't you think?" I asked.

"It looks that way. Monica could be right, but all I can go on is what I see and can prove. I'm sorry, but I don't have the luxury of guessing," Sam said with a shrug of his shoulders.

"I understand. I've been there, but I've always had to try to out-guess what was going on. I still tend to do that," I admitted.

"I did find out something else. I had the police look over Mr. Holcome's room. The blood they found in Jeff's room was not Jeff's."

"How do you know that?"

"Jeff Holcome's blood type is on file at Games Unlimited. He was a regular blood donor at the company's blood drives. The police tested the blood. Jeff's blood is a different type than that found on the sheets."

"I think you should have the blood found on the towels and sheets checked against Tilman and Whitman. If it's theirs, then we know for sure that they were killed in Jeff's room," I explained.

"We are already doing that, but I don't have the results back, yet," Sam replied.

"Do you think both of them were killed in Jeff's room?" Monica asked. "How would he get them out of the hotel without being seen?"

"That's a good question," I said as I tried to think.

Now things were getting really confusing. What happened in that room? Had Jeff actually killed Tilman and Whitman in his room, then taken their bodies out to the car? It was certainly possible, but how did he get them to his car without someone seeing him. There was always the possibility that he used a service elevator. If he took them out of the room in a laundry cart or something like that, no one would have paid any attention to him.

"By the way," Sam said interrupting my thoughts. "I also found out who the head of security at General Dynamics is. I talked to him shortly after I talked to you this morning. He said he knows nothing about Mr. Holcome except that he delivered a software disk to them as scheduled."

I looked at Monica and she looked at me. This changed everything. If Jeff had delivered the disk as he was supposed to, then why was everyone looking for him?

"It seems that he called them from the airport and asked them to wait so that he could get the disk to them right away.

They waited for him, and he delivered it the same evening he got here," Sam explained.

"That explains why he seemed to feel better after he made his phone call from the airport," I said as I looked at Monica.

"Nick, what is going on?" Monica asked, the look on her face showing how confused she was.

"Honey, I don't know," I replied as I looked toward Sam.

"Did the head of security at General Dynamics give you any idea what the software disk was for?" I asked Sam, hoping that I would get some sort of an answer, but not really expecting one.

"Yes. He said it was to repair a minor glitch in their accounting software. It was nothing more than a repair disk. It had nothing to do with anything remotely considered to be secret."

"We've got several people looking for Jeff. He already delivered the disk to General Dynamics. What is it Jeff has that they want so badly that they would risk so much to find him? And if Jeff did kill Tilman and Whitman, what was he trying so hard to protect?" I asked, again more to hear myself think.

"His system for winning at Blackjack," Monica suggested as a possible answer.

I looked at her. It was as if it took a moment for it to sink in, but she was probably right. The only other thing I could think of was maybe a new game that Jeff had developed.

"You might very well be right. But there's always the possibility that they're after some other new game or games he has developed," I added to give them something more to think about.

"That might be possible," Sam added. "But have you thought of this? It might be both. They could be one in the same."

"What are you getting at?"

"Suppose your man thinks he developed a game that would make it possible for almost anyone to win at Blackjack?"

That was certainly an interesting thought, but I felt it had several holes in it. The idea needed to be looked at just the same.

"Okay. Let's look at what we know. Jeff came here to test a system he developed to win at Blackjack. He played at several different tables in several different parts of the casinos. He won a lot more than he lost. Doesn't that prove his system might work?" I asked looking at Sam for an answer.

"Not really. Blackjack is a card game. It would be impossible to shuffle the cards exactly the same way each and every time, unless you cheated. In order for any system to work, there would have to be some things that could be counted on to happen the same way, every time, all the time. In cards, that is not possible unless the cards are stacked.

"The only thing a system might be able to do is to make the odds a little better, a little more in the player's favor," Sam explained. "But remember, the odds would still be in the houses favor. Over the long run, he would lose."

"Could he have developed a way to at least improve the odds?"

"I guess it's possible, but I don't see how. Granted, I'm no computer expert, but those who are experts have spent years trying to figure the odds of winning at any given game, including Blackjack.

"Even the best computers in the country can't beat the odds over a period of time. There is no way to set up a system that will beat the house over the long run without cheating, like stacking the deck, or in this case, fixing the computer to create certain parameters. By setting the limits of the parameters, you are, in fact, stacking the deck. In games of chance like those in casinos, the odds are in favor of the house. That is what the house is counting on to make its profit," Sam said with a note of confidence."

"Assuming that what you say is true, and I'm sure it is, the people after Jeff are really after a new game he developed, or at least they think he has developed," Monica injected.

"You're probably right," Sam said as he looked from her to me.

"If that's the case, why was Jeff dressed like a woman?" I asked.

"Either it wasn't Jeff, or he knows that the house security is watching him and he doesn't want them to know it's him," Monica suggested.

"Give this a try. Maybe he knows someone is after his new game and he doesn't want them to find him. Maybe it has nothing to do with house security at all," I suggested.

"That's certainly possible," Sam agreed. "As long as there is no indication that he was cheating, we would have little or no interest in him. My guess is that he probably knows that."

We finished our lunch with little additional discussion. I was deep in thought. The more we tried to figure out what Jeff was up to, the more questions we had without answers. It was becoming clear that we had to find Jeff before anyone else found him.

No matter how hard I tried, I had no idea what Jeff's next move might be. In fact, I had no idea what my next move was going to be at the moment. The only thing I knew for sure was that I didn't want anyone dogging my tail, especially Boyer. I knew that when Monica and I left Knollwoods, I would need to lose Boyer and his friends as quickly as possible.

Just as we finished eating, I noticed a security guard coming toward us. He had a piece of paper in one hand and a cell phone in the other. I watched him as he gave the note to Sam.

After Sam read the note, he took the cell phone from the guard and dialed a number. He turned away as he talked on the phone. I could not understand what he was saying, but he was sure interested in whatever he was being told.

When he was finished, he turned back toward us. Looking at me, he pushed a button on the cell phone and laid it on the table.

"That was a friend of mine with the police. He said they found the rental papers for Jeff's car in Barbara Whitman's purse. It appears that Jeff had loaned her the car while he was here."

"Do you think Jeff knows that the car was found with a dead body in it," Monica said with surprise.

"If he doesn't know about the dead body, he doesn't know that someone is looking for him," I added.

"He would have to know. What about the blood in his room?" Sam asked.

"If he didn't know about the blood in his room, he could be in more danger than he knows. If he does know about it, I have to wonder just what is going on," I said.

"Could it be that he doesn't know that Tilman was killed in his room?" Monica asked.

"I guess it's possible. If Tilman came to his room after he checked out and was found there by someone looking for Jeff. It's possible that Tilman was mistaken for Jeff and they killed him. The room could have been ransacked in an effort to find the disks," I suggested as a possible scenario of what might have happened.

"If we take the approach that he doesn't know about any of this, I'd be willing to bet that he has no idea what is going on around him," Monica suggested.

"Why would he?" Sam asked. "Didn't he come here to test his system at Blackjack? Didn't he deliver the disk to General Dynamics on time?"

Sam made a good point. The big question was, does he really know what was going on and he is in it up to his neck;

or he is completely unaware of what is happening around him as Monica suggested?

"I think one thing is for sure. I'd be willing to bet that he doesn't know that his wife called the hotel looking for him. As far as he knows, no one has even missed him. If it hadn't been for his wife calling you, we wouldn't be here looking for him now," Monica said.

"If, and I say if, he doesn't know what is going on, he's running around playing Blackjack without a care in the world. As far as he knows, the only people he is ducking is Casino Security. He probably is only ducking them because he doesn't want them to know he has a system," I said with a grin.

"In that case, little does he know that his life is at stake," Sam added.

"Yes, but he will find out. I hope not too late," Monica said, her concern showing in her voice.

"I'm having a great deal of difficulty believing that he doesn't have at least some clue to what is going on. In fact, I think he is in this up to his neck," I said as I thought about our discussion.

"You might be right. Either way, I think Jeff is in trouble. There are people out there looking for him who want what they think he has. No matter what we think, Jeff's life expectancy is not looking very good at the moment," Monica said.

"You are right about that. I think we'd better find him and find him fast," I said.

"Where are you going now?" Sam asked.

"We're going to the only place that we know he is scheduled to be at, his hotel in Hartford," I replied. "If he doesn't show up there, then I think there's a good chance we won't find him alive."

Monica looked at me. Her lovely cobalt blue eyes told me that she was afraid that Jeff might already be dead. I would almost be willing to agree with that assessment. But before I was ready to assume the worst, I had to make every effort to find him.

I pushed back from the table. After thanking Sam for his help and the lunch, I took Monica by the arm and led her out of the café. We returned to our room and began to pack. As I was putting my shaving kit together, I stopped and turned to look at Monica. She was packing her things as well.

"Monica?"

"Yes," she replied as she stopped and looked at me.

"If we walk out of here with our bags, whoever is watching us is going to know that we are leaving."

"That's true," she replied as she straightened up and dropped what she had in her hands on the bed.

"I think we should just leave everything here and go to Hartford without it. We can pick up what we need there. We can come back here and pick this up later," I suggested.

"I think that's probably a good idea."

"I'll call Sam and ask him to keep our room open for us."

Monica nodded in agreement. I walked to the phone and talked briefly with Sam. He agreed with us and told me that he would hold our room if I promised to keep him informed as to what we found out. He seemed genuinely concerned about Jeff's well being. I promised that I would give him a full rundown on everything when we returned. He was also kind enough to make arrangements to get us out of the hotel unnoticed.

After we put our clothes back in place so it looked like we were still staying here, we went downstairs to the floors where the casinos were located. We walked through one of the casinos and slipped out a side door with the help of one of the guards Sam had sent to help us get out without being seen.

Once we got to our car, we left and headed south toward the Mystic and Groton areas. I made several stops at various places to make it look like we were simply sightseeing, just in case someone had seen us leave. It gave me a chance to make sure that we were not being followed. As soon as I was convinced that no one was following us, I turned north and headed toward Hartford.

CHAPTER TEN

It was around four in the afternoon when Monica and I arrived at the hotel in Hartford where Jeff was scheduled to stay for his conference. After parking our car, we entered the front lobby and walked toward the front desk. I wasn't sure if we would find Jeff here or not, but this was the place where he was supposed to be for the conference and for the next couple of days.

As we approached the front desk, I noticed that there was a man in his mid-to-late fifties watching us. He took time to look us over rather well as we approached the desk. From the look on his face, I was sure that he was curious about the fact that we didn't have any luggage. The fact that Monica was younger than I, and I might add much prettier than I, probably didn't help his thoughts about us any.

When I stopped at the front desk, he looked at me with an artificial sort of smile, the kind that lets you know that he is there to help you if you don't ask too much of him. One of those smiles that makes you wonder if the poor man had had his prune juice for breakfast.

"May I be of assistance?" he asked, sounding a little bit uppity.

"Yes, as a matter of fact you can. I would like to know if you have a Jeffery Holcome registered here?"

"Oh," he replied with a note of surprise, then looked toward the computer screen as he typed on the keyboard.

I was sure that he thought we were going to ask him for a room. With no luggage, I could just about imagine what he was thinking. Of course, it didn't matter to me what he thought.

"Yes, sir. Mr. Holcome checked in just a little over two hours ago."

"Great. Would it be too much to ask what room he is in?"

"He is in room 316. Would you like me to call his room and tell him who is calling?"

"No, I would not."

The man just stood there and looked dumbfounded at me. It was apparent that he had expected me to say yes to his question. The surprised look on his face was one for the books. I almost laughed out loud.

"I've known Jeff for many years and I'm a friend of his wife. I want this to be a surprise," I said with a smile.

"Oh, I see."

I knew darn well that he didn't see at all, and I sure wasn't going to explain it to him. Monica and I turned and walked away from the desk leaving him to wonder what was going on.

"That wasn't very nice of you," Monica said with a grin.

"I know, but I wasn't going to explain to him why we are here. It's none of his business."

"I know. Are we going to Jeff's room?"

"For starters, I think that would be a good idea. I'd like to know if Jeff is really here."

Monica didn't say anything more. She simply took me by the arm as we walked to the elevator. Once we were in the elevator, I pushed the button for the third floor. We waited silently for the doors to close and for the elevator to move to the third floor.

When the doors opened again, we found ourselves standing face to face with Jeff. It was apparent by the look on his face that he was surprised to see me standing only a few feet in front of him. But I had to give him credit for his quick recovery.

"Well, imagine meeting you here," Jeff said, a big smile replacing the surprised look.

"Yeah, quite a surprise isn't it," I said as he stepped back so that we could step off the elevator.

"What brings you here?" Jeff asked. "Are you into computers?" he asked with a grin.

Jeff seemed a little nervous at seeing me. His eyes darted from me to Monica, then back to me.

"No. We are here to see you," I replied bluntly. "Let's go to your room. We need to have a little talk some place private."

Jeff looked from me to Monica, then back at me again. He started to say something, but must have decided against it. Instead, he turned and led us down the hall to his room. Once inside Jeff's room, he closed the door and pointed toward a couple of chairs.

"Have a seat, please," he said politely.

Monica and I walked across the room and sat down on the chairs next to a small round table. Jeff walked over to the bed and sat down on the edge of it.

Since he looked a little confused and moved rather slowly, I got the impression that he was delaying any conversation we might have for as long as possible. It was almost as if he felt a little trapped and needed a few minutes to compose himself, especially his thoughts.

"Well, now, I don't believe that I know your friend," he said with a smile as he turned and looked at Monica.

It was clear to me that he was stalling. There was no question that we had caught him off guard.

"Jeff, this is Monica Barnhart. Monica, Jeff Holcome."

"Nice to meet you," Jeff said forcing a smile. "Sharon said you were very pretty and she was right."

"Thank you," Monica replied.

"Speaking of Sharon, she is the reason we're here," I said in a matter of fact tone.

"Oh. Why is that? I mean, ah, I don't understand."

"Sharon tried to get hold of you the evening you left Chicago. When the front desk told her that you had not checked in, she got worried."

"What? Is something wrong?"

Jeff suddenly seemed concerned that there might be something wrong at home. Yet, I got the impression that it might also have been an act. I also got the impression that he had no idea that Sharon liked to keep close tabs on him.

"There is nothing wrong at home except that Sharon is a worrier, and she is worried about you. She has to know where you are at all times," I said.

"I never found her to be that way," Jeff replied with a slight defensive tone in his voice.

"You were never late for dinner, always at home in the evenings and on weekends, and always called her if you had a change of plans. Am I right?"

"Yes, I guess that's true," he agreed after taking a moment to think about what I had said.

"Sharon tried to call you to make sure that you had arrived safely. When you weren't here, she got worried and called me. She asked me to find you."

"That's ridiculous," he blurted out.

"No, that's what happened," Monica assured him. "She had no idea that you were going to Knollwoods Resort and Casino to play Blackjack before the conference."

Jeff looked at Monica. It was clear to me that he thought his little side trip to the casino was a well kept secret. Now the secret was out of the bag. From the look on his face, this bit of information changed everything. He had the appearance of a little boy who had been caught with his hand in the cookie jar. He acted as if he was not quite sure just what to say.

"I . , . I"

He stammered around, probably trying to figure out what he should say next. Although he acted as if he was feeling guilty for not telling Sharon that he was going to do a little gambling, I got the impression that he was more interested in how much we knew about his little side trip to the casino. I decided that I would not let on that we knew anything other than the fact that he did a little gambling at Knollwoods.

"It's fine with me if you want to take a couple of days away from home to play a little cards or spend some time in front of a slot machine. I don't really care and it's none of my business. But it might be a good idea if you let someone know."

"I did let someone know," he replied.

"Yeah, but you should have let your wife know, not your secretary," I explained.

"Did my secretary tell you where I was going?"

"As a matter of fact, yes. She told us that you were going to play a bit of cards before the conference. She was worried about you, too," I replied.

"Why would she worry about me?"

"Maybe it's because she cares about you," Monica said, as she looked him in the eye.

Jeff looked at her. I'm sure that there was no doubt in his mind that Monica knew that he and his secretary had something more between them than a simple working relationship.

Jeff was beginning to look really worried now. I had to wonder if Monica had guessed right about his relationship with his secretary.

"Listen Jeff. I don't care what you do, but when you draw so much attention to yourself it tends to bring on problems."

Jeff turned and looked at me. The expression on his face was hard to read, but I got the feeling that he might not know what I was talking about. He either didn't know what was happening, or he was a very good actor. The more I studied his reaction, the more I tended to believe the latter to be true.

"Why would playing a little cards draw so much attention, as you put it?" Jeff asked.

His question and the look in his eyes gave me the feeling that he was looking for more than just a simple answer. It was more like he was trying to find out just how much we knew about his activities. I wasn't about to tell him everything we suspected.

"Your secretary told us that you had a system for winning at Blackjack, and that you were going to test it at Knollwoods Resort and Casino. Have you given any thought that there might be someone else who might be interested in your system?"

He seemed very nervous and hesitated before answering.

"Who?"

"I don't know, but winners at casino tables always become of interest to others. They either want to know how you do it, or they want to be around when you pick up your winnings."

"I don't have a system for winning at Blackjack. I'm working on a new Blackjack computer game. I was doing some research on it. I wanted to know if the game was true to life. That's all," he said, but a nervous twitch in his right eye hinted that what he was saying might not be the whole truth.

"I'm sure that you know how much Sharon is opposed to gambling. I didn't want her to get upset with me for going to a casino," Jeff added.

"You mean all this is over a game that you are working on?" I asked, acting as if I had no idea what was going on.

"Yes. What did you think it was about?"

"Well," I said, then paused as I quickly thought about what I should say next. "I guess I didn't really know, but you have caused a lot of worry for Sharon as well as your secretary."

Jeff's nervousness seemed to dissolve and he looked at me as if he had no idea what I was talking about. His response to what we had told him was what one would have expected from someone who knew nothing about what was going on, but there seemed to be a slight hint of relief in his posture.

He sounded very convincing, but I was not ready to believe him. There was just too much pointing in his direction for me to believe that he didn't know what was going on. The fact that he had dressed as a woman the last day he played Blackjack at Knollwoods was enough for me to suspect something wasn't right. He may not have killed Tilman and Whitman, but there was little doubt in my mind that he was hiding something. The only thing bothering me was the fact that I didn't know what it was he was hiding.

There was more to this than what was on the surface. I could see it in his eyes. Than again, it just might be my suspicious nature.

"Jeff, what are your plans now?" I asked.

My sudden change of pace seemed to set him back a little. He stared at me for a moment or two before answering.

"I have several seminars and workshops to attend over the next couple of days, and a speech to give tomorrow evening."

"Then what?"

"When the conference is over on Monday, I'll go home early Tuesday morning," he said as a matter of fact.

"You're not going back to Knollwoods Resort and Casino?"

"I hadn't planned on it. Why?"

"I take it that you have completed the testing of your game?" Monica asked.

I realized from Monica's question that she had some doubts about him, too. Even as convincing as he sounded, I don't think she was buying into his story any more than I was.

"Yes," he replied as he looked from Monica to me, then back to Monica.

I was sure that there was nothing more that we were going to get out of him without laying all our cards on the table. I wasn't ready to do that, not just yet. To do that would tip him off that we thought there was something going on other than just the testing of his new game. There was no doubt in my mind that he knew more than he was admitting. The only real question was just how much did he know and how much of this was he involved in?

"I think you should call Sharon and let her know that you are all right. She's worried about you," I said.

"I'll do that. I'll call her right now, if you will excuse me."

I looked at Monica and noticed that she was looking at me. She shrugged her shoulders. We had done as much here as we dared. It was time for us to leave.

"Come on, honey. We should leave him to call Sharon," I said as I stood up.

I took Monica by the hand and walked toward the door. As I reached for the doorknob, I looked back at Jeff and saw him watching us. He smiled and reached for the phone. I nodded as if to say, "You're doing the right thing," then turned and left his room.

As the door closed behind me, I wondered if he really would call Sharon, or if his show of picking up the phone was just to convince us that he was going to call. I had my doubts.

If he was as smart as I believed he was, he would call her just to get her off his back for a few days. That would be enough time for him to finish his business, whatever his business was. I was sure that it was not the conference.

"Did you believe him?" Monica asked as we started down the hall to the elevators.

I gave her question a good deal of thought. Jeff had played his part well, but I wasn't buying it. He had to know something was going on. After all, I didn't think of him as stupid.

"No. I think when this conference is over, maybe before, he will either return to Knollwoods for a few days or he will suddenly disappear completely."

"You think he is getting ready to disappear?"

"I don't know for sure, but I wouldn't rule it out as a possibility."

"What do we do now?"

"We find out what seminars and workshops Jeff has signed up for. We need to find the registration desk for the conference."

We returned to the front desk in the lobby and found out from the desk clerk where those attending the conference had to go to register. The woman at the registration desk was very pleasant and very helpful. She provided us with a complete schedule of the events and a list of the seminars and workshops that Jeff had signed up for. After we had as much information as we felt we could get, we left the hotel.

Just down the street was another hotel. We drove down there and checked in. As soon as we got to our room, I went to the bed and sat down on the edge. Monica sat in a nearby chair while I picked up the phone to call Sam Bradford at the Knollwoods Resort and Casino.

"Hello, Sam. It's Nick McCord.

"How's it going?"

"Good. We found Jeff alive and well."

"Great. I had my doubts if you would find him alive. Have you talked to him?"

"Yeah."

"What did he have to say for himself?"

"Nothing."

"Nothing?" Sam asked in surprise.

"Yeah. He acted as if nothing was wrong. I still think there's something going on, but I can't figure out what it is. I want you to keep an eye out for him in case he shows up there again. We are going to stay here for a couple of days and see if he keeps his schedule at the conference."

"Sure, no problem. I'll alert my people."

"Great. Anything going on down there I should know about?"

"Boyer came by. He wanted to see the videos of Mr. Holcome. I told him that since the woman that was killed in the parking lot was on the tapes with Mr. Holcome, the State Police had impounded the tapes. I told him that they would not be available for several days."

"Good thinking. I'll get back to you later."

After I gave him the phone number of where we could be reached, I hung up the phone. I looked over at Monica. I could tell by the look on her face that she wondered what I was grinning about.

I told Monica about what had happened at Knollwoods Resort and Casino since we left. It interested me that Boyer was still looking for Jeff at Knollwoods. With all his connections, I would have thought that he would have followed Jeff here. But then, maybe he had someone else following him, and probably us.

"Nick?"

"Yeah, honey?"

"What do you think is going on with Jeff? What do you think he is doing?"

"I don't know. One thing that keeps haunting me was his reaction to calling Sharon."

"I don't understand."

"When I mentioned that Sharon had sent us to find him, he seemed very worried that something was wrong at home. Yet, when we suggested that he call her, he didn't seem that interested."

"I still don't understand."

"That's just it, I don't either. I think we need to keep an eye on him as much as we can. I get this feeling that he will suddenly disappear."

I was still sitting on the edge of the bed as I looked at Monica. She stood up and came over to the bed. I laid down on the bed and she joined me. She curled up against my side and rested her head on my shoulder. I tucked her up close to me.

We lay quietly together. I guess we were deep in our own thoughts. It seemed to me that the more we found out, the less we seemed to know.

The fact that Jeff had delivered the disk to General Dynamics on schedule without any hang-ups struck down the theory that he was being followed because someone wanted the disk that he was to deliver to General Dynamics. It was clear that this was not a spy case, at least not one that involved the government or military secrets.

I was feeling tired, but I didn't really want to go to sleep. I had too many questions running through my mind for that. The one major question was what was Jeff up to? I had to wonder if he knew what he was doing. If he did, I had to wonder if maybe he had gotten in over his head.

It seemed the more I thought about Jeff, the more I realized that I still don't know him very well. I had no idea what it was that made him tick.

Time seemed to drift by as I lay on my back looking up at the ceiling. With Monica's head on my shoulder, my thoughts drifted to our original purpose for being here. We had come here simply to find Jeff. That much we had accomplished. But deep down inside I knew there was more that we had to do. I could not drop it here. Two people that had been with Jeff recently were now dead. I needed to find out why.

As I thought about Monica curled up beside me, I began to wonder what we were getting into. Maybe we had gotten in over our heads, too. I was beginning to think that maybe I was putting Monica in danger by insisting that we work together.

There were already two people dead that had some sort of a connection to all this. The only thing was that I couldn't figure out what the connection might be. Maybe if I knew what was going on, I would be able to figure out how they were involved and why they were now dead?

Suddenly, Monica stirred beside me. I looked over to see her looking up at me. Her beautiful blue eyes drew me to her. As our lips met, she pressed herself up against me. We kissed passionately. All I knew at that moment was that she was the one woman in the world for me.

She slowly moved back away and looked into my eyes.

"Did you get any rest?" she asked softly.

"No, not really."

"Thinking about Jeff?"

"Sort of."

"Me, too," she replied.

"What do you think?"

"I think he's in big trouble."

"I agree, but what are we going to do about it?"

"I don't know. I don't know if there is anything we can do," Monica said with a sigh.

"I agree. I think all we can do is to watch him and see what he does. I have a feeling that he will return to Knollwoods."

"Why? Why would he return there?"

"To cash in his chips and maybe try to win a little more?"

"If he believes that he has a winning system, why wouldn't he just go to another casino where no one knows him and win himself a new pot of money?" Monica asked.

One thing I learned about Monica was that she could ask some pretty hard questions. She knew I didn't have the answers, but it helped me to think about it.

"He has several thousand dollars worth of chips from there. Something about him tells me that he is not all that willing to give them up," I said thoughtfully. "He will go back there, it's just a matter of time. He may just stop off long enough to cash in his chips, but he will go back there."

"Are you sure?"

"No, not really. It's just a gut feeling. I get the impression that he's not the type to just let several thousand dollars go."

"In other words, you think he is greedy?"

"Yeah," I replied as I thought about it. "That was just what I meant."

"You might be right," Monica said as she laid her head back on my shoulder.

"I think we should go out to dinner, then go over to the conference and see if Jeff actually attends the seminar tonight that he signed up for," I suggested.

Monica agreed with me so I rolled off the bed and got ready to go. As soon as Monica was ready, we went down to the main floor of our hotel and had a relaxing and very pleasant meal in the hotel restaurant.

Most of our conversation during dinner was speculation on what Jeff was doing. We had a lot of theories, but nothing concrete to support any of them. We needed something, some small clue that would lead us in the right direction.

After dinner, we returned to the hotel where the conference was being held. Having the schedule of events, we were able to find the conference room where the seminar that Jeff was scheduled to attend would be held.

We went to the room and peeked inside. We could hear the voice of the speaker as he droned on about some part of computer programming that I couldn't understand. He might as well have been speaking in a foreign language for all I understood.

It didn't take us long to find Jeff sitting at a table watching the speaker. He seemed to be making notes on a pad, but from where we were it was hard to tell for sure.

"Well, he's here," Monica said.

From the sound of her voice, it came across as if she was disappointed. I had to wonder if she might have expected him to have disappeared again.

"Yeah."

"What now?"

"The schedule indicates that this seminar lasts until about nine tonight. It's just seven-thirty. I doubt that he will go anywhere tonight. He's pretty smart. He will expect us to be watching him at least until tomorrow. Plus, he would know that we couldn't get a flight out until tomorrow anyway.

"If we make ourselves scarce, he may get the idea that we have left and have gone back to Chicago. I would like to have him think so," I added.

We left the hotel where the conference was being held and started to walk back to our hotel. I held Monica's hand as we walked. It was a pleasant evening.

"Do you think he'll call Sharon?" Monica asked as we walked along.

"I would think so. He'd be pretty stupid if he didn't. He already knows how much trouble she has caused him by just not knowing where he was and what he's doing."

"If what you say is true, wouldn't it be a good idea if you called Sharon and told her that we found him? You could also tell her we're going back to Chicago, then on to Madison tomorrow," Monica said with a hint of a grin on her face.

It didn't take a genius to figure out what was on her mind. If Sharon called Jeff, or he called her again, she would most likely tell Jeff that we were returning to Chicago or Madison. He might even buy it. If he did, that would make it easier for us to follow him. He would not expect us to be around. This was one smart woman.

"You are good. I like the way you think," I said as I squeezed her hand.

I led Monica into our hotel and across the lobby to the elevators. As we rode the elevator to the floor our room was located on, I thought about what I would say to Sharon. I wanted her to believe that we were coming back to Chicago so that she would tell Jeff, but I didn't want to make it sound like there was any kind of a problem.

We went directly to our room. I sat down on the bed and picked up the phone. As soon as I had an outside line, I dialed Sharon's number.

"Hello?"

"Hi, it's me," I said trying to keep an upbeat tone in my voice.

"Oh, hi. Jeff called me. He said you found him," she said, her voice sounding more up beat now.

"Yeah. I was just checking in with you to make sure that you had heard from him."

"I'm sorry that I sent you on a wild goose chase. He told me that he went early to the conference so that he could meet with a friend of his that was in the computer business. Jeff wanted to test some game he was working on and wanted his friend's opinion. He ended up staying overnight with him in some place called Mystic."

"Good, I'm glad he called you."

"He said that he had some people waiting for him. He was going to have dinner with them, then listen to some speaker talk about something to do with computers. I don't understand those things. He said he was going to call again tonight, after a seminar."

"That's good. Well, I guess Monica and I will leave here in the morning. We have some business to take care of in Madison."

"Nick?"

"Yeah?"

"Thanks for your help. I really am sorry that it was for nothing," she said, the tone of her voice showing how much she meant it.

"That's all right."

"Goodbye, Nick."

"Goodbye, Sharon," I replied, then hung up the phone.

Monica sat in a chair waiting for me to say something. I'm sure that she knew something good was going on because of the grin on my face.

"Well," she insisted.

"She said Jeff called her and is going to call her again after the lecture he is attending tonight."

"Great."

"You are one smart lady," I said as I watched her stand up.

Monica walked across the room and stood in front of me. I looked up at her.

"I'm glad you see more in me than just a pretty face," she said in her sexiest soft voice.

"You are definitely more than just a pretty face," I said as I reached out to her.

As I lay back on the bed, I pulled her down over me. I wrapped my arms around her and kissed her. She returned my kiss. The next few minutes were spent kissing and hugging.

It wasn't long before we were undressing each other. We spent the next hour or so making love to each other. Afterwards, we took a shower together and then climbed into bed for a good night's sleep.

CHAPTER ELEVEN

I woke rather early in the morning, long before the sun came up. Monica was still sound asleep next to me. I didn't want to disturb her, but I had too much on my mind to just lay there and be still. I carefully slipped out of bed and went over to the window. As I sat down on the windowsill, I drew back the curtain a little and looked out. It was still dark, but the street below was lit up by the streetlights. I noticed that there were very few cars on the street at this hour.

I watched as a street sweeper moved along the street next to the curb like a large bug gobbling up everything in its path. It darted out from the curb only to avoid a parked car that was parked directly below the window, then quickly darted back in along the curb again and continued to move along.

Although it was interesting to watch what went on in the predawn hours in the city, it was not what was on my mind. The actions of Jeff were my preoccupation at the moment. I had too many unanswered questions. My mind was so full of them that sleep was out of the question.

One thing that kept coming to mind was the death of David Tilman. Who was he, and what did he have to do with Jeff? All we knew about him was that he might have worked for Games Unlimited at one time, but that had not yet been confirmed. We also had a pretty good witness that placed him at an inn in Mystic with Barbara Whitman the evening before he was found dead.

I had seen both Tilman and Whitman on the surveillance tapes from Knollwoods Resort and Casino. On the tape they did not appear to know each other. Yet, there was a strong possibility that they had been at the inn in Mystic together.

The only other thing I knew for sure about them was the fact that they were both dead. What I didn't know was why they had been killed and by whose hand.

Although I had been looking at a car that was parked across the street from the hotel, I had not really been watching it. However, my attention was suddenly drawn to it when I noticed a light go on inside the car. The light stayed on for only a few seconds before it went out again.

My attention was now focused on the car. At first I thought that someone might have gotten in or out of the car, but I hadn't seen anyone in the street or on the sidewalk. It was then that I realized what it was that I had seen. There was someone in the car who had just lit a cigarette. I watched carefully in the hope of seeing something else, but nothing else happened.

It didn't take a great deal of brain power to figure out what was going on. Whoever was in that car was on surveillance. They were watching someone, or waiting for someone to leave the hotel. I had to wonder if they might be watching for us. If they were, they could end up sitting there for a very long time. Since I knew they were there, it would not be all that difficult for us to leave by another door.

Once I had put the car out of my mind, at least for the time being, I again turned my attention to Jeff. There just seemed to be too many things that happened for Jeff not to be aware that something was going on. I had to wonder if he knew about the deaths of Tilman and Whitman.

My thoughts turned to Jeff's rented car. How was it that Tilman's body was found in the car Jeff had rented at the airport? Yet, Whitman had the rental papers in her purse? The one possible answer that came to mind was that Whitman and Tilman had both been killed at the same time, or very close to the same time. Neither one of them had been killed where they were found.

The evidence, however slim, pointed to at least one of them having been killed in Jeff's room at Knollwoods Resort and Casino. Whoever killed them, dumped her body in the trees near the parking lot and took Tilman down the road several miles and dumped him, along with the car, at the cemetery. The only question I had was why?

If they had been killed at the same time, did the killer think that by putting them in different places that no one would connect the two murders? That hardly seemed likely as both of them had been killed with a small caliber handgun, probably a .22 or .25 caliber automatic, and in the same manner. If I had to guess, they were killed by the same person or persons.

Could it be that the rental papers for the car were in Whitman's purse to lead investigators away from Jeff? The only reason that I could come up with for the bodies to be in two different places when there was such a high probability that they had been killed at the same place was simple. The car Jeff had rented did not have a big enough trunk to hold both of the bodies.

My thoughts were disturbed when I heard Monica roll over in the bed. I turned to look at her. In the dim light of the room she looked as sexy as any woman in the world. I had to grin at myself. Here I was sitting on a windowsill thinking about dead people when not fifteen feet away was a beautiful and sexy woman lying naked in a hotel bed, and she was very much alive.

"What's the matter, honey," Monica said, the sound of her voice showing that she was still only half awake.

"Nothing. I just couldn't sleep."

"Come back to bed. It's too early. We can sit down in the morning and talk about it."

"Yeah," I replied as I stood up and walked across the room.

She held the covers up for me and I crawled in beside her. She quickly rolled up against me, resting her head on my shoulder.

Within a few minutes she was sleep again. I knew what I had to do in the morning. I needed to make a couple of phone calls. I needed to find out who Tilman and Whitman were, and who Boyer was. We needed to clear up who was working for whom. If I could do that, I would probably have half my questions answered.

With the feel of Monica's warm body up against my side, I found that I could put my thoughts of Jeff and what he was up to aside, at least for a little while. I then found it easier to drift off into a restful sleep again.

* * *

When I woke again, the sun was trying to peek in around the edge of the curtains. It cast a glow over the room. Monica was still lying beside me, but I could tell that she was awake, too.

"Good morning," Monica said softly.

"Good morning."

"You ready to get up?"

"Yes."

Monica sat up and looked down at me. She had a worried look on her face.

"What were you thinking about last night?"

"I was trying to figure out who Tilman and Whitman were."

"That is the third or fourth time I've heard you do that."

"Do what?" I asked.

"You put their names together like you think they might belong together."

I hadn't thought about that, but she might be right. It had not really occurred to me, but then why not? The lady at Whaler's Inn indicated that they were husband and wife. I had to wonder if that might be the case. It would not be the first time that a couple used different last names to keep others from knowing that they were married.

"You might be right. Didn't Tilman have a Games Unlimited ID card on him, or at least in his wallet?"

"Yes, he did," Monica answered.

"I think a call to Games Unlimited is in order."

"You think he might have really worked for them?

"Maybe. It's obvious why Boyer didn't know him. He was not working for Games Unlimited. I can only think of one way to find out why Tilman had an ID card for Games Unlimited, and that's to call them and ask."

Monica nodded her head in agreement as she thought about it. I sat up, leaned over to her and kissed her lightly. I then turned around and swung my legs over the side of the bed.

With Monica kneeling on the bed behind me, I reached over and picked up the phone. I dialed the number for Games Unlimited's switchboard. The phone only rang a couple of time before it was answered.

"Games Unlimited, how may I direct your call?"

"I would like to speak to the head of security, please."

"Just one moment, I'll connect you."

I waited while the call was transferred.

"Mr. Springfelt's office, may I help you," another woman asked.

"I would like to speak to Martin Springfelt, please."

"May I ask who's calling?"

"Nick McCord."

"Just one moment, Mr. McCord."

I wondered how long I was going to have to wait before she would come back and want to know what I wanted to talk to him about. Suddenly, the phone was answered.

"Mr. McCord, this is Martin Springfelt. Have you been able to find Jeff?

"As a matter of fact, yes I have."

"Where did you find him?"

"We found him right where he was supposed to be, in the hotel in Hartford at the computer conference."

"What? I don't understand. I received a called from Sam Bradford at the Knollwoods Resort and Casino. He told me that Jeff was there."

"He was, but he is here in Hartford at the computer games conference now."

"I'm glad to hear that. We were worried about him," Martin said, the tone of his voice indicating that he was genuinely worried about Jeff.

"He delivered the repair disk to General Dynamic as scheduled, but he stopped off to test a new game he was working on."

"To test a game? I don't understand."

"I'm not sure we do, either. But that's not the reason I called you.

"You're wondering if you will get reimbursed for your expenses?"

"No. Well, sort of," I replied.

"No need to worry, Mr. McCord. Games Unlimited will reimburse you for all your expenses and will pay you your going rate when you submit a bill," Martin said without a moment's hesitation.

"Thank you, but that is not the reason I called."

"Oh. Is there a problem with Mr. Cooper? I told him to give you any assistance that you required."

"No, sir. Mr. Cooper has been very cooperative. I was wondering if you were able to find out anything about a man named Boyer, Kenneth Boyer? We're not even sure that's his real name."

"No. Mr. Bradford asked me to look into him. I haven't been able to find anything on him here. What is your interest in him?"

"Let's just say that he was looking for Jeff, too. He told me that he works for you. In fact, he said that he was the Chief of Security."

"He certainly doesn't work for us. Only you and Mr. Cooper are working for us. Do you have any idea why he would tell you that?"

"No. I have another reason for calling you. Do you know a man by the name of David Tilman?"

"David Tilman was one of our security people."

"What do you mean 'was'?"

"He was fired about a month to six weeks ago. I can get you the exact date, if you need it."

"No. That won't be necessary. What was he fired for?"

"It was believed that he was stealing secrets of some of our games that were under development. We were never able to prove it, but we decided that it was best to confront him with it before we lost too much. When we did, he resigned."

"So he really wasn't fired?"

"Well, not really. But he would have been if he hadn't resigned."

"Do you know who he might have gone to work for after he left Games Unlimited?"

"No. As far as I know, he is still unemployed. Why do you ask?"

"He was found dead a couple of days ago."

"Oh. I'm sorry to hear that."

Martin sounded as if he was truly sorry that Tilman was dead. However, I found it interesting that he didn't ask any questions about the cause of his death.

"What do you know about a woman by the name of Barbara Whitman?"

"She works in the game development section here. Why?"

That piece of news came as a bit of a surprise. She worked in game development, and Tilman was accused of stealing programs from that very department. With Jeff working in that part of the company, there was little doubt in my mind that they all knew each other. There was also the possibility that they knew each other very well.

"Do you know where she is now?"

"If you can wait just a moment, I can probably find out."

"I'll wait."

As I waited on the phone for several minutes, I could hear him punching keys on a computer keyboard. I got the impression that he was looking for her schedule.

"It appears that Miss Whitman is currently on vacation."

"Do you happen to know where?"

"No. I wouldn't have any idea where she would go for her vacation."

"Can you tell me when she is due back?"

"She took a two week vacation, and it looks like she has been gone for just about a week. I would think that she should be back to work a week from Monday. What is your interest in her?"

"Just a name that came up. I like to check out everything I can. I don't like loose ends."

"I see. Is there anything else I can do for you, Mr. McCord?"

"No, I don't think so. I'll be in touch," I replied, then hung up the phone.

I turned and looked over my shoulder at Monica. I could tell by the look on her face that she had heard all of the conversation. I wondered if she had gotten the same message that I got.

"Interesting," I said.

"I agree," Monica replied. "I have a question."

"What's that?"

"Why didn't you tell him that Barbara Whitman was dead?"

"For the same reason I didn't get into Tilman's death. I didn't tell him how Tilman died and he didn't ask. That tells me that there is a strong possibility that he already knew that

Tilman was dead. And if that's the case, he might very well know that Whitman is dead, too."

"Why wouldn't he have told you that he knew Tilman and Whitman were dead?"

"A very good question, but I don't have a very good answer."

"Do you think he might be involved in some way?"

"Possible, or it could more likely be that he is so used to keeping quiet about things that he just didn't think I needed to know. But on the other hand, he might not have known about Tilman's death until I told him, and he may not know of Whitman's death. He probably doesn't get very much Connecticut news in Chicago. As far as we know, nothing has been on the news about either of them."

"I'm sure you're right. He probably wouldn't have heard about it yet."

"I think we need to get dressed and get something to eat. I also want to check and see if Jeff attended this morning's seminar session."

"Okay. I am kind of hungry."

I gave her a light kiss, then stood up. I went into the bathroom to take a quick shower. I no more than got into the shower when Monica stepped in with me.

"You mind?" she said softly wearing nothing but a sexy smile on her face.

"No," I replied as I pulled her up to me and took her in my arms.

Monica tipped her head back as I leaned down to kiss her. The feel of her body pressing against me cleared my mind of everything but her. I slid my hands over the silky smooth skin of her back. There was nothing in this world that was more important to me than the woman in my arms.

We spent the next half hour or so enjoying the warmth and freshness of the water running over us. We took this time to show our love for each other and to share the bar of soap.

When we were done, we dried off and got dressed. We took the elevator to the main floor of the hotel and went into the restaurant for morning brunch.

When we were finished, we started for the front door of the hotel. I remembered the car parked across the street and stopped.

"What's the matter?" Monica asked.

"There was a car parked across the street last night. I think they were watching this hotel."

"You think they were watching for us?"

"Could be."

"What do we do?"

"We go to the hotel where Jeff is and check on him. Then we return here, get the car and go to the airport," I explained. "If we're being followed, we might as well let them see us go."

Monica nodded that she understood. I took her hand and we walked out the door. I looked around as if I was trying to decide which way to go.

I noticed the car parked across the street with two men in it. They acted as if they hadn't seen us. But as soon as we turned and started to walk toward the hotel Jeff was staying at, one man got out of the car.

When I would turn my head to talk and glance at Monica, I would also glance across the street toward the man at the same time. I didn't recognize him. At the moment, I wasn't sure who it might be. There were two possibilities that I could think of. It was either one of Boyer's men, or it was one of Cooper's men. Either way, I wasn't about to take any chances, although I doubted that it was one of Cooper's men.

The thought of a third possibility crossed my mind, but I had no idea who it might be. If there was a third party, it meant that we would have to be ready for almost anything.

"We've got a tail."

"Any idea who?"

"No, but it doesn't matter. We're still going to make it look like we are returning to Chicago."

Monica just grinned at me. I was sure she had figured out what I had in mind.

"Just in case the car is bugged, don't say anything that might even hint that we are not returning to Chicago," I said as we turned into the lobby of the hotel.

"Do you think it might be bugged?

"I don't know, but they have had the opportunity to bug it. It sat in the hotel garage all night," I explained as we walked across the lobby toward the conference rooms.

When we arrived at the conference room where this morning's seminar was to be held, we stopped at the door and looked inside. There, in the same chair that he had been in when we left last night was Jeff. He was taking notes and paying very close attention to the speaker. In fact, he looked so engrossed that it almost looked like an act.

"Looks almost too perfect," Monica said.

I had to agree with her. My gut feelings told me that he was up to something. It made me wonder how long Jeff would continue the charade. How long before he would break away from the conference and do whatever it was he was going to do. The only problem I had was not knowing what he was doing, or when he was going to do it. One thing I was convinced of was that he would not leave the conference until after he gave his speech.

"Are you satisfied?" Monica asked as she turned and looked at me.

"For the moment. Let's go to the airport."

Monica and I turned around and left the hotel. We walked back to our hotel, checked out and went to the garage to get the car.

As I drove out of the hotel garage and onto the street, I noticed the dark sedan still parked across the street. It wasn't long before I noticed that same car following us at a distance. It stayed about the same distance behind us all the way to the airport.

When we pulled into the car rental return area, I saw the sedan drive on by. But when we were done checking in the car; and we were about to board a shuttle bus to the airport terminal, I saw the car drive by again. It didn't look as if they were going to follow us into the terminal.

I was sitting in a seat that allowed me to see out the rear of the shuttle bus by looking in the driver's big overhead mirror. I didn't see any cars that looked like they were following the bus. However, when the bus stopped to let us out at the terminal, I saw the same car was stopped at the curb ahead of the bus.

Monica and I walked into the terminal. I didn't see anyone get out of the car, which gave me a little breather. I didn't know how far we could carry out this little act. We didn't even have tickets to fly back to Chicago.

At this point, I was about to turn and go over to the car rental counter and rent another car. A quick glance around told me not to stop yet. I saw a man who seemed to be watching us. I wasn't sure if he was one of the men from the car, but I couldn't take the chance.

I guided Monica toward the ticket counter where we purchased two tickets to Chicago. Once I had the tickets and boarding passes, we went to the security checkpoint that leads to the boarding areas. We were quickly cleared through security and began walking on down the concourse to the boarding area.

"What happens when they see that we don't board a plane?" Monica asked.

"I hope it doesn't go that far. If he's carrying a gun, it might be a little difficult for him to follow us past security."

"This is one time when I hope he's carrying a gun," she said.

At this point I couldn't have agreed with her more. I glanced up at a large overhead mirror. The man was standing on the other side of the security checkpoint watching us. I let out a sigh of relief.

"He's not following us," I assured Monica. "We'll go to the departure gate and wait there until the plane leaves. Then we'll go rent another car."

I walked along the concourse holding Monica's hand feeling a little better about things. We arrived at the gate where the plane for Chicago would be departing. We found a couple of seats in the corner and sat down. I was tired already, and I was sure that Monica had been feeling the tension as well. I tipped my head back and closed my eyes.

I hadn't been resting my eyes for more than a few minutes when I heard something on the overhead television. I could hear a newswoman talking.

"The body of David Tilman of Chicago Heights, Illinois, was found in the trunk of a rental car behind the stone wall of an old cemetery near Ledyard Center. A spokesman from the police department indicated that there was evidence of foul play. It is not known at this time if the man found in the trunk of the car is the man who rented the car."

"I guess that's out," Monica said with a long sigh.

"Yeah. Now all we have to do is wait to hear about Miss Whitman."

"Why do you think that they leaked out Tilman's death, but not Whitman's?

"That's a very good question."

"Do you think it might have to do with the fact that Whitman's body was found on tribal land?" Monica asked.

"I don't know, but if Sam is able to keep it under wraps for a little while, all the better. I need more time to figure out what's going on."

Monica didn't say anything more. I didn't close my eyes again and try to rest any more, either. I kept an eye on the news. I was hoping that we wouldn't hear about Miss Whitman's death.

Thinking of her made me wonder about Jeff. Miss Whitman was an employee of Games Unlimited. Since she worked in the game development section, there was a strong possibility that she knew Jeff long before he 'met' her at Knollwoods Resort and Casino. If that was the case, why did they pretend that they didn't know each other? What were they trying to hide?

There was also a very strong possibility that Jeff knew Tilman. Did the three of them have some sort of deal in the works? If they did, what was the deal and what went wrong?

I knew that I had no answers, but I had plenty of questions. I also knew that none of them were going to get answered here. The thought passed my mind to get up and leave, but to leave before the plane left might mean that we would lose what little advantage we had going for us.

"Nick?"

"Yeah, honey?"

"I just had a thought. What if that guy is still waiting for us outside?"

"Well, I guess this little 'hide and seek' game will have been for nothing."

"Are we going back to Hartford?"

"I don't think so," I replied after giving it a little thought. "I think we'll go back to Knollwoods. We'll get Cooper to follow Jeff."

I could see by the look on Monica's face that she was thinking about what I had said. Seeing the grin come over her face gave me some assurance that she agreed with my idea.

"You could call him from here," Monica suggested.

It was a smart idea. That would give Cooper the chance to get here hopefully before Jeff split for parts unknown.

"Wait here, I'll be right back."

I got up and found a pay phone. I placed a call to Cooper. The phone was answered immediately.

"Cooper Investigations," the woman's voice said.

"This is Nick McCord. I would like to talk to William Cooper."

"Just one moment, Mr. McCord."

It was less than a minute before Cooper was on the phone.

"What can I do for you, McCord?"

"You still working for Games Unlimited?"

"Yeah. They told me to give you all the help I could."

"You know who Jeff Holcome is?"

"Yeah, sure."

"I would like you to put a tail on him. I would like your best man. I don't want to lose him."

"I'll do it myself. Do you know where I can find him?"

"He's at the conference in Hartford. He gives a speech tonight. I've got a feeling he's going to try to disappear after the speech, maybe tonight, maybe tomorrow morning."

"I'll get right on it. Where can I contact you?"

"You can contact me through Sam Bradford at Knollwoods Resort and Casino."

"Okay. Anything else?"

"No, not at the moment. Keep in touch. Let me know where he goes and who he talks to."

"Will do."

I hung up the phone and went back to the gate where I had left Monica. She was sitting there looking at me as I approached her. The look on her face told me that she was interested in how things went. I sat down next to her and told her about my call. We then waited until the plane outside the window started to move away from the building.

We walked along the concourse back into the terminal. We made a stop at the ticket count to turn in our tickets for reimbursement, then on to the car rental booth.

The woman at the booth gave us a rather strange look. I was sure she was wondering what we wanted.

"Hi," I said with a smile. "I would like to rent a car."

"But you just turned in the car you already had rented."

"I know, but I would like to rent another car."

"I can give you the same one you had, if that's all right?"

"No. I prefer a different car. One of a different color at least."

"Yes, sir," she replied, but the look on her face indicated that she thought my request was very strange.

As she started filling out the papers, she glanced up at me and then at Monica. I got the feeling that she thought we were just a little off balance.

"If you don't mind my asking, sir, was the car you had not satisfactory?"

"No, not at all. I would just like a different car."

"Yes, sir," she replied timidly.

As soon as she finished the paper work and I signed the forms, we took the keys and left the airport. When we got to the car, we found that she had rented us a deep red Chrysler 300. When Monica saw the car, she looked at me.

"I guess it pays to ask for a different color," I said with a grin.

Monica just smiled and got in. After closing the door for her, I got in and started the car. We left the airport and started back toward Knollwoods Resort and Casino.

CHAPTER TWELVE

We arrived at the Knollwoods Resort and Casino just shortly after one in the afternoon. I drove the car to the front of the building where we got out. One of the valets parked the car in the garage while we went inside.

Our first order of business was to find Sam Bradford and see if he had any new information for us. As we walked through one of the casinos, I noticed that nothing seemed to change around here. It seemed to always be busy, yet there was always a slot machine that wasn't being used or an empty stool at one of the table games that a customer could find and where he could spend his money.

When we arrived at Sam's office, his secretary greeted us. After she announced our presence, we were directed into Sam's office.

"Good to see you back," Sam said as he stood up behind his large oak desk and gestured for us to sit down.

"How did things go in Hartford?"

"I think a little better than expected, but not as good as we would have liked," I replied.

I could see by the expression on Sam's face that he didn't understand what I was getting at. To help him understand, we sat down and I told him about our meeting with Jeff at the hotel. When I got done explaining what had happened, he sort of agreed with us that something didn't seem right.

"I don't know what Mr. Holcome is up to, but I've got something that you might find interesting. Just before noon, a woman came in and began cashing large numbers of chips. She cashed over two thousand dollars worth of them at the cashier's booth in the Grand Pequot Casino, then another two thousand dollars worth at the cashier's booth in the Rainmaker Casino. When she finished there, she went on down to the Smoke Free Casino and cashed an additional nine hundred dollars worth of chips there."

"That's about what we figured that Jeff had left with," Monica said as she looked at me.

"Yes. But who was the woman?" I asked as I looked at Sam.

"I don't know, but we have her on tape. I tried to call you in Hartford to let you know about her, but you had already checked out of the hotel. I had a hunch that you were on your way back here."

"You didn't happen to catch her, did you?"

"No. I'm afraid that I couldn't do that. First of all, she had done nothing wrong. The chips were ours and we had no choice but to pay her for them. As long as we could not prove that they were stolen, our hands were tied."

"Damn."

I knew it might help if we could identify the woman, but I would have preferred to have had the chance to talk to her in person.

"We weren't able to hold her, but there is one bit of good news, however," Sam added with a reassuring grin on his face.

His comment quickly caught my attention. And by the look on Monica's face, it had caught hers as well.

"When she left, I had her followed. She went directly to the Two Trees Inn. She used part of the money to pay for a room for three more days. Two Trees Inn is just across the road."

"What do you mean, 'three more days'?"

"The room was originally registered to a William Grant for just three nights. She registered as Mrs. William Grant and told the clerk that she was to meet her husband there and wanted to extend the stay for three more days."

I looked at Monica. I was looking to her to see if the name rang any bells with her. It certainly didn't with me. It was clear by the expression on her face that the name didn't mean anything to her, either.

"Are you still keeping an eye on her?" I asked.

"Yes. I have one of our people watching her. She hasn't left the room since she checked in. She gets all her meals brought in. If she does decide to leave, I have instructed our people to let me know immediately and to follow her."

"Good. Could we see the video tape of her?"

"Certainly. It should be here shortly. I already asked security to bring it to me as soon as they had isolated the parts that would show her."

"Great. Any idea how long it will take?"

"It shouldn't be much longer. I had them start working on it as soon as I found out about her. I have one other bit of news that you might find interesting."

"What's that?"

"The night desk clerk at the Two Trees Inn was shown a picture of Jeff Holcome taken from the video. He identified the man in the picture as William Grant. I also found out that he checked into the Two Trees Inn the same night he left here."

"So that's what happened to him after he checked out of here and before he showed up in Hartford," Monica said.

I had to agree with Monica, but now there was another woman that seemed to be connected to Jeff. I wondered who it was. I also knew that there was nothing we could do about her at the moment. I felt we should at least look at the tapes before we went to see her in the hope of identifying her.

"Have you heard anything more about Boyer and who he is?" Monica asked.

"So far, Martin Springfelt has not been able to find out anything about him. I had a picture made of him from one of our surveillance cameras. It caught him as he passed through one of the casinos. I sent the picture to Springfelt in the hope it would help him identify the man."

"I take it you have not heard back from him?"

"No, not yet. I sent it only about an hour ago."

I had no idea where Boyer was from, but he had followed us from Chicago. That could mean that he might be from that area. The thought crossed my mind that I might be able to get some help from one of my old friends. I still had a friend or two on the Milwaukee Police Department. If I sent a picture of Boyer to them, they might be able to come up with something on him. I knew it was a long shot at best, but I had nothing to lose.

"Would you be willing to send a copy of that picture to a friend of mine?"

"Sure. No problem. Who would you like it sent to?"

"The Milwaukee Police Department. I'll have to call them first and get their fax number."

"You're welcome to use my phone. I'll go see if that video is ready," Sam said as he stood up and left Monica and I alone in his office.

I placed a call to an old friend of mine, Sergeant Frank Wallace of the Fifth Precinct of the Milwaukee Police Department. I explained my problem to him. He told me to fax the picture to him. He said that he would do what he could to find out about the guy and let me know as soon as possible. I got his fax number, then gave him Sam's fax number and the number of Sam's office in case he wanted to get in touch with me.

After a brief update on what I was working on, I thanked Frank and hung up the phone. I sat down next to Monica and told her that Frank was going to do what he could.

"Do you think he will be able to identify Boyer for us?"

"I don't know, but it's worth a try. If I know him, he'll send the picture on to the Chicago Police Department and see if they can come up with anything. Frank is a good man. We've been friends for a good many years."

Just then Sam returned from the outer office. He had a videotape in his hand.

"I have it," he said as he walked over to the television and the VCR recorder. "If you're done with your call, we can look at it."

"I'm done. Would you please ask your secretary to fax the picture of Boyer to this number?"

"Sure thing."

Sam took the number I had written on a piece of paper along with the picture of Boyer to the outer office. Within a minute or two he returned. He turned on the television and started the tape. Monica and I watched with a great deal of interest.

When the video began to play, I saw a woman standing in line at the Cashier's booth. She had a large plastic container that looked like one of those cups used for big drinks that are sold at convenience stores. She held it tightly against her chest as if it was extremely valuable, which by all reports it was. Her motions gave me the idea that she might be a little nervous. She kept looking around, as if she was afraid someone would see her. Unfortunately, she kept looking away from the surveillance camera.

For the first few minutes of the tape, I could not see her face. When it was her turn to cash in her chips, she poured the chips on the tray and pushed them under the glass. I couldn't get a good look at her face as she kept her head tipped down.

She was watching the cashier very carefully as the money was counted out. When the cashier pushed the money out to her, she quickly pushed the money deep into her purse. It wasn't until she turned to leave the cashier's booth that she turned and looked almost directly toward the camera. It was then that I got a chance to see her face.

"It's Janet Marshall," Monica said with surprise.

"It sure is," I agreed.

"You know this woman?" Sam asked, he seemed a little surprised.

"We sure do. The woman is Jeff Holcome's personal secretary. We talked to her in Chicago before we came here," I explained.

"She is the one who told us that he was coming here," Monica added.

Monica was right. Why would she tell us he was coming here if she was going to be here? She knew that we were looking for Jeff. She had to know that we would follow him here. It didn't make any sense.

"Do you think she's in on this?" Monica asked me.

"I have some serious doubts that she was in the beginning. If she had been, she would never have told us that he was coming here," I said.

"Why do you think she's here now," Sam asked.

"I think Jeff called her and had her come here to cash in his chips for him. I think he thought we would either be on our way back to Chicago, or that we would still be in Hartford. I don't think he expected us to come back here so soon."

"That makes sense. That could also explain why she hasn't left her room since she checked in," Sam said as he thought about it. "She might be afraid that the two of you might see her if you did return here."

"What about the videos? He had to have thought about that. After all, he did try to dress up like a woman so he could play Blackjack without being recognized," Monica said.

"Well, we're still not a hundred percent sure that it was him. But even if it was, I doubt that he thought that anyone would be looking for a woman cashing in some chips," I replied.

"What is this woman to Mr. Holcome?" Sam asked.

"For one thing, she is his secretary," I said.

"I think she is more than just a secretary to him. I think they have something going between them," Monica added.

"You think they're lovers?" Sam asked.

"Possibly," Monica replied.

"If not, she is so in love with him that he can get her to do just about anything for him," I said as I continued to watch the video.

I sat back in the chair and began to wonder how deeply Miss Marshall was involved. She seemed genuinely concerned for Jeff's safety when we visited with her at Games Unlimited. Now here she was cashing in the chips that Jeff had won. Then it hit me like a brick on the head. Jeff already knew that Miss Marshall had put us onto him. He knew that she had told us about his side trip to Knollwoods. In fact, we told him that she had told us.

"Jeff must be pretty confident that we went home, or that we would stay in Hartford as long as he was there. Otherwise, he would have to be very stupid to let Miss Marshall cash in his chips for him," I said almost more to hear myself think.

"He would have to trust her a great deal," Sam added.

"Yes. And she would have to be very attached to him to do it for him," Monica said, adding her thoughts.

"I have to wonder just how much Miss Marshall knows about what is going on. I've got a feeling that she doesn't really know what Jeff is up to," I said.

"Nick, do you think Jeff is just using her?" Monica asked.

"My guess would be, yes. She is so devoted to him that she would do almost anything for him, and I think he knows it. I also think he is taking advantage of her feelings for him."

"I have to agree with you on that, Nick," Sam said.

"She's going to get hurt. I can feel it," Monica said in a soft sympathetic voice.

"I'm sure of that. I just hope she doesn't get herself killed over this. We already have two dead bodies that can be traced back to Jeff. One more will not mean anything to him," I added.

I had to think about what Monica had said. There was no question in my mind that Miss Marshall was going to get hurt. If nothing else, she was going to get emotionally hurt. I only hoped that would be all. I was sure that she had no idea what she was getting herself into, and how much danger she could find herself in.

"What's your next step?" Sam asked interrupting my thoughts.

"I think it's a wait and see situation right now," I replied. "I don't want Miss Marshall to know we are here. At least not yet."

"Don't you think we should let her in on what has been happening? After all, her life might be at stake here," Monica said.

Monica had a good point. The only problem I had with it was that if we let her know what was going on, there was a good chance that she might tell Jeff. If that happened, there was no telling what Jeff might do. He might just drop everything and return to Chicago as if nothing had happened, or he might just up and disappear. My bet was on the last one, especially if he had killed Tilman and Whitman.

"You might be right, but I don't think we can risk letting her know that we are watching for Jeff. Not yet, anyway." I said.

"I could put a guard on her," Sam suggested.

"Without her knowing?"

"Sure."

"Then do it."

The offer of a guard made me feel a little better about not telling her. At least someone would be watching over her. If worst came to worst we could tell her what we knew, but for now it was best to keep it from her.

I watched as Sam called someone. I heard his part of his conversation as he set it up so that Miss Marshall would be protected, but I wasn't really listening. My mind was cluttered with my own thoughts of Jeff and what he was up to.

After Sam had finished his call, we all sat quietly in Sam's office. It was as if we were waiting for something to happen.

From the looks on Monica and Sam's faces, they were as deep in thought as I was. It seemed that there was nothing we could do for now but to think and try to figure out what Jeff's next move might be. It was wait and see time.

The ringing of Sam's phone suddenly disturbed our thoughts. Both Monica and I watched as he picked up the phone.

"Yes," Sam said into the receiver.

We waited as Sam listened.

"One moment, please," Sam said then he held the phone out to me.

I took the phone from him and put it to my ear. I had no idea who might be on the other end.

"Hello?"

"Nick, my boy, this is Frank."

"Hi. Got anything for me?"

"Sure do. You wanted some info on this guy you call "Boyer"?"

"Yeah. You got something on him?"

"He's a smart one, this fella'. It seems that he's been arrested in Milwaukee and Chicago on several occasions for extortion and industrial espionage. The most time he has spent in jail was a couple of nights. It seems that all his witnesses have either turned up dead, refused to press charges, or just plain disappeared. Plus he's got one hell of a good lawyer. We can hardly get the paperwork done before his lawyer springs him. What have you gotten yourself into this time, Nick?"

"I am not sure, but what you just told me makes we wonder."

"By the way, his real name is Kenneth Boyer."

"You're kidding?"

"Not at all."

"Why do you think he used his real name?" I asked.

"He's pretty cocky. By the way, he's also very dangerous. You be careful."

"I will, and thanks, Frank."

"Good luck," Frank said then hung up.

I looked across the desk at Sam as I hung up the phone. I was sure that he could see the worried look on my face and wondered what I had found out.

I sat back in the chair and looked down at the floor as I gathered my thoughts. My concern for Monica was growing with each moment that I thought about who we were dealing with. Although I had not intended to, I had put her in danger. More danger than I had expected.

"Well," Monica asked impatient to hear what I had found out.

I turned and looked at Monica. After taking a deep breath, I began telling her and Sam what Frank had told me. I had to admit that I was hoping that she would want to give it up and return to Madison, but I knew her better than that. She would stick it out to the very end, regardless of what the end might be.

"At least now we know who Boyer really is," Monica said after thinking a moment or two about what I told her.

"We do know that," Sam replied. "But what is he after? What is it that Jeff has that he wants?"

"My guess would be he wants the computer game that Jeff developed," I replied.

"Do you think Jeff is trying to sell the game to the highest bidder?" Monica asked.

Sam and I looked at her. What she said made a good deal of sense. But if Jeff was dealing with the likes of

Boyer, his life wasn't worth a nickel. I began to remember what I had heard about how a company could become a big success or a total failure overnight because of one computer game. If that was true, then the computer game that Jeff had developed could be worth a lot of money to another computer game company.

With all the people that were following Jeff, I had to believe that there was more than one person, or company, that was after his game. Still with the strong possibility that Tilman, Whitman and Jeff all knew each other, and Tilman having been fired for suspicion of stealing components to games under development, I felt that there was a strong possibility that Jeff was trying to sell his game to one of Games Unlimited's competitors.

Obviously, Games Unlimited wanted the game back. That was clear by the fact that they had hired Cooper Investigations to find Jeff.

Jeff was on Games Unlimited's payroll. According to the law, that meant any games he developed for them belonged to them, not to him. They had all the rights to the copyrights and the profits that might be made from the sale of such games. That would explain why they wanted to find Jeff, and why Cooper had been looking for him.

But who was Boyer working for? He had to be working for someone. That was clear from what Frank told me about Boyer having been arrested for industrial espionage. I could see no reason for the likes of Boyer to want the game except for what he could make by selling it to someone else.

"Nick, what are you thinking?" Monica asked.

"I have a good idea what Jeff is up to," I replied.

"You mind letting us in on it?" Sam asked.

"I would be willing to bet that Jeff is trying to sell the game he developed to someone."

"He can't do that. Games Unlimited has the rights to it," Sam said.

"I know, but Jeff might feel that he is not getting what he deserves from Games Unlimited. After all, his game could bring Games Unlimited millions of dollars. All he would get out of it would be his salary, and maybe a bonus."

"Then you think he is trying to get the money for himself?" Sam asked.

"Sure. Jeff would not be the first person to invent something for the company he worked for, then try to sell it to a competitor even though he has no legal rights to it."

Sam nodded that he agreed with my assessment of the situation. I looked over at Monica to see what she thought. She looked like she didn't think it might be that simple. The more I watched her think about it, the more I began to think that she might have something else on her mind.

"Honey, what are you thinking?"

"I was thinking that Jeff might be wanting to sell the game to another company as you suggest. But I think Boyer is in it for something else."

"Like what?"

"Like a winning system to Blackjack," she suggested.

I had to admit that she did have a very valid point. I could see Boyer working for someone else, but I could also see him working for himself. If he thought that Jeff had a winning system, Boyer could probably see nothing in front of him but dollar signs.

"I think she might have a point," Sam said.

"You might be right."

"What do we do about it?" Monica asked.

"I don't know. I think we have to wait until Jeff makes his next move."

"I sure hope that Cooper doesn't lose him," Sam said.

I couldn't have agreed with him more. I had this gut feeling that if we lost Jeff this time, we would never see him alive again.

As I saw it, there was little chance that Jeff would leave the conference before he gave his speech. His speech was scheduled for seven o'clock tonight. That would mean that he would not be able to get back here to meet Miss Marshall before nine or ten o'clock this evening, if he left right after his speech.

"Sam, I want you to tighten your surveillance of Miss Marshall starting no later than nine o'clock tonight."

"Okay."

"Do you expect Jeff to come here right after his speech?" Monica asked.

"I don't know, but I figure that is the earliest that he could get here if his speech takes about an hour. I don't know if he will come here tonight or sometime tomorrow, but I think he will come. Miss Marshall has his money, and I have a feeling that the money is his traveling money."

"You think he's going to split from here?" Sam asked.

"I think it's a possibility, a strong possibility."

"I'll get on it right away," Sam said.

As Sam reached for his phone, I stood up. I reached out for Monica. She took my hand and stood up.

"Where will you be?" Sam asked as he put his hand over the mouthpiece of his phone.

"In our room," I replied as I turned to leave.

I slipped my hand around behind Monica and guided her to the door. Once outside Sam's office, we started to walk down the hallway toward the elevators that would take us to our room.

"What next?" Monica asked.

"We have several hours before we will know if Jeff is returning here. I would like to go to our room. I need time to think."

"Okay."

"There's something we are missing, something that we have not thought of," I said as we stepped into the elevator.

"What do you mean?"

"Our answers to the questions we have come up with still leave a few things unanswered. I need some quiet time, some time to think."

"Would you like me to go somewhere while you think?"

"No. I want you with me. You may have some of the answers. I need you to help me think. There's got to be something we're missing."

Monica just looked at me. I was sure that she was wondering what I was getting at, but she was kind enough not to say anything. The problem was that I didn't know what I was getting at myself. It was more of a gut feeling than anything else. I had to work it out. Over the years I had found that some quiet time to just think undisturbed was often what it took for me to see things in a clearer, or even a different light.

As soon as we got to our room, I laid down on the bed. I stretched out with my hands behind my head. Monica joined me on the bed, only this time she did not roll up against me. She lay quietly beside me. I think she was waiting for me to say something, but I had nothing to say.

I closed my eyes and let my mind wander. There was something that was not fitting in the picture. It reminded me of that old question, "what's wrong with this picture?" That was the question that I needed to answer before anything else would make sense. There was something wrong and for some reason I couldn't see it.

"Monica, what do you think of Jeff?"

"Oh, I don't know. He seems a bit strange to me."

"What do you mean?"

"Well, he doesn't act like he's worried about the things you would expect him to worry about. For example, he didn't ask us anything about who was following him. I don't know, but he just didn't seem to respond the way I thought he should have to us."

"I understand what you are saying. He sounded phony, like it was all an act to get us out of the way," I replied.

"There's another thing that disturbs me. He didn't once mention the fact that his rental car was missing. It was as if he already knew and didn't care."

"I can't see how he could not know that it was missing. My best guess is that he not only knew it was missing, but he knew where it was and how it got there," I said.

"You think he might have killed Tilman and Whitman?" Monica asked.

"I'm certainly leaning that way."

"But why?"

"The oldest reason in the world, greed."

"He doesn't seem the type," she said.

"What type is a murderer?" I asked even though I knew what she really meant.

Monica didn't reply, but then a reply was not needed. I think we were both thinking that we might have misjudged Jeff.

"Nick, I think I'll take a short nap if you don't mind."

"I think I will, too."

I closed my eyes as I laid beside her. I was still thinking of Jeff and trying to figure out what his next move might be. I was sure that he was going to return to Knollwoods Resort and Casino to meet with Miss Marshall. He would probably collect his money from her, but what he would do after that was yet to be discovered.

CHAPTER THIRTEEN

I wasn't sure just how long I had slept, but I suddenly found myself wide awake and staring at the ceiling. The sun was still up as I could see it trying to shine in around the edges of the closed drapes.

I turned my head and saw that Monica was still napping beside me. She was curled up on her side with her back to me. I didn't want to disturb her so I rolled over to the side of the bed and sat up. Monica stirred slightly, but didn't wake up.

Suddenly the phone rang. I tried to reach over and pick up the receiver before it woke Monica, but I wasn't quick enough. She rolled over and looked at me as I put the receiver to my ear.

"Hello."

"Is this Mr. McCord, Nick McCord?" the voice on the other end asked.

"Yes, who is this?"

"Mr. Bradford would like you to meet him in the security monitoring room as soon as possible."

"Tell him I'll be there in a minute," I said and hung up.

"What's happening?" Monica asked.

"I don't know. Sam wants me to meet him in the monitoring room right away. So hurry up and get ready."

"You go on ahead. I'll catch up with you there," Monica replied as she sat up.

"Are you sure?"

"Yes, silly. I'm a big girl. I can find my way. You get going."

I leaned over and gave her a kiss. I was a little reluctant to leave without her because of all that had happened over the past few days, but she was right. She was a big girl.

"Go. It could be important," she insisted.

I smiled at her and then started for the door. As I got to the door, I turned around and threw her a kiss. She winked and smiled, and then I turned and left the room.

Before going on down the hall, I made sure that the door had locked behind me. I then went on down the hall to the elevators.

It seemed like it took forever for the elevators to arrive. As soon as it did, I moved closer to the door. As I stepped toward the elevator, I had to stop to let a man wearing a gray sport coat get off the elevator. As soon as he was out of the elevator, I got on.

I really didn't take much notice of the man. He seemed to know where he was going, and I had other things on my mind.

When the elevator arrived at the floor I wanted, I got off and headed directly to the door that led into the narrow hallway and onto the security monitoring room. When I got to the door, it was locked. I looked around for a security guard, but there was no one in sight.

My first thought was that if Sam had wanted me in the security monitoring room, he would have known that I didn't have a key to the door. He would certainly have sent a guard to wait for me so that I could get in.

I began to wonder what was going on. I reached out and knocked on the door. Maybe the guard was on the other side of the door and was simply waiting for me to knock, but when I knocked there was no answer.

I turned and looked around. My mind was still trying to figure out what was going on. I noticed a phone on the other side of the hall. I started toward it with the idea of calling Sam's office, but before I went more than a couple of steps I saw Sam walking toward me. He smiled as he approached. He didn't seem to be in any hurry.

"Where's Monica?" he asked sort of casually. "I'm not used to seeing you without her."

"She'll be down in a minute. What did you want?"

"What do you mean?" he asked as a puzzled look came over his face.

"You had one of your people call me and tell me to meet you here."

"No, I didn't. I didn't call for you."

I looked at him. Now I was the one who looked puzzled. What was going on? My mind suddenly filled with questions. Then it hit me. Someone wanted me out of our room, but why?

"Monica!" I said as I turned and started running back toward the elevator.

Sam must have thought that I had totally lost it, but he followed right on my heels. I didn't look back to see if he was following me because I could hear him running behind me. I could also hear him talking on his two-way radio as we ran toward the elevators. He was asking for guards to go to our room immediately.

When we arrived at the elevators, one opened just as we got there. We ran into it and I pushed the button to the floor that our room was on. The elevator doors didn't seem to want to close. I pushed the button several times in an effort to get the doors to close. Finally, the doors closed and the elevator started to move. I was impatient to get back to our room.

One look at Sam told me that he knew what I was thinking. I could see the worried look on his face.

"Come on, come on," I said as I looked up in the hope that the elevator would move faster.

When the bell rang and the elevator doors opened, I dashed out and turned down the hall toward our room. Sam was still close behind me.

When I arrived at the door to our room, I found the door was slightly ajar. I barged into the room and found Monica sitting on the edge of the bed. She looked at me with a surprised look on her face.

"What's the matter?" she asked as she looked at me as if I had lost my marbles.

"I thought they had gotten to you," I said as I breathed a sigh of relief.

"What are you talking about?"

"When I got down to the main floor, I ran into Sam," I said as I tried to catch my breath. "He said that he didn't call for me. I guess I got worried and thought, well, I thought you might have been kidnapped."

"I'm fine. No one has been here," she reassured me.

"But the door was unlocked. I distinctly remember making sure it was locked when I left," I said.

"Oh, I heard someone at the door and I thought you might have left your key behind. When I got to the door, whoever knocked on the door was gone. I didn't bother to lock the door again as I was almost ready to leave anyway," Monica explained.

Suddenly, the phone began to ring. I took a deep breath to settle my nerves, then reached over and picked up the receiver.

"Hello," I said as calmly as possible.

"Listen very carefully. I'm only going to say this once. I just wanted you to know that you cannot protect your lady friend all the time. You get my meaning?"

"I get your meaning," I replied as I looked over at Sam. "What do you want?"

"Very perceptive. I want Jeff Holcome and the disks, and you're going to get them for me. I will call you in exactly twenty-four hours. If you don't have Jeff or the disks, your lady friend will not be with us very long," the voice on the other end said.

I was about to respond, but the phone went dead. I looked at the receiver as I slowly hung up the phone, then I looked at Monica, then at Sam. I was well aware of what a person could do if they were motivated enough. No one is safe from an assassin if he really wants to kill someone.

"What was that about?" Sam asked.

I could see the seriousness in the lines of his face. He knew there was something going on.

As I glanced over at Monica again, I could see the worried look on her face, too. I knew that I had put her in danger by bringing her here.

I told them about the caller and what he had said. Sam looked down at the floor for a second before he looked up at me again.

"First of all, we have to put a guard on Monica at all times," Sam said.

"That won't be necessary. I don't plan to let her out of my sight until this is over," I stated flatly.

"Okay. I want you to think. When you came rushing down to see me, did you see anyone around here?

I took a minute to think before answering him.

"There was a man that got off the elevator just as I got on to go down."

"What did he look like?" Sam asked.

"I'm trying to think. I looked at him, but I didn't really look closely. Give me a minute," I said as I closed my eyes and tried to picture the man in my mind's eye.

"He was about six foot tall, weighed about two hundred to two hundred and twenty pounds. He had dark brown hair with brown eyes, I think. His face was sort of pockmarked. He was wearing a gray sport coat, dark pants, black I think, a white shirt and no tie."

"Did he look at you?"

No, I don't think so. He might have, but I don't remember seeing him look at me."

Sam put his two-way radio up close to his mouth and quickly reported a complete description of the man to all his security guards. When he finished he looked at me.

While he was working on getting a description of the man that I had seen out to his security people, I was trying to place the voice that I heard on the phone. There was something remotely familiar about it, but I couldn't quite place it.

"What's wrong?" Sam asked disturbing my thoughts.

"I was just thinking that I've heard that voice before. I just can't figure out whose voice it is."

"Someone you heard just recently?"

"I'm not sure. Say, can you trace that call? Can you at least tell me if the call was made from inside the hotel?"

"No, I don't think so. I would had to have a tap on your line, but even then I don't think he stayed on the phone long enough to trace it."

Suddenly, I had a thought. The call might not have been made inside the hotel. I hated to think that I was that predictable, but then I did just what most people would do under the circumstances. If that was the case, it could mean that someone could have placed the call from outside the hotel to me. But the more I thought about it, the more I realized that someone had to have been here to know that I left the room without Monica.

"Sam, would you be able to find out if any calls were made from, say, this hotel to another hotel such as Two Trees Inn. Or from, say, Two Trees Inn to this room?"

"I might. What are you getting at?"

"Whoever made that call knew that Monica had been left alone. Someone had to tell the caller. That would most likely have been the man that I saw in the hall. And they knew that I had returned to the room. Again someone had to tell them, probably someone downstairs near the elevator. If the call came from outside the hotel, then my guess is that the guy I saw coming out of the elevator might be our link to whoever it is who wants Jeff and his disks."

"It's a hell of a long shot, but I'll see what I can do," Sam said.

Sam immediately got on his two-way radio and called the desk. I knew I was reaching for the sky on that one, but it was a possible lead that might help me figure out who was after Jeff and his disks. If the call had been made from Two Trees Inn, it may have been made from Miss Marshall's room.

"Sorry, Nick. No calls to the front desk and no calls that I can trace to anyplace else," Sam said, his voice showing his concern and disappointment.

"I knew it was a long shot, but I couldn't think of anything else," I said.

"Let me call Two Trees Inn. Maybe they know if anyone called out from there to here."

Sam didn't wait for a response from me. He simply picked up the phone and called the inn. It took him several minutes before he got an answer, but it proved fruitless, too.

Suddenly, I remembered that Cooper was supposed to be tailing Jeff. I glanced at my watch. If Jeff's speech had lasted about an hour, than he could have already left the hotel in Hartford. The problem I had was that there was no real hard evidence that Jeff was going to come here. The only clue that we had that he might return to this area was Miss Marshall. She had checked in and paid for three more days. It was still a guess on our part as to whether or not she would actually stay the three days.

"Sam, do you still have guards watching Miss Marshall?"

"Yes."

"Good. If Jeff Holcome shows up, I want to know immediately."

"Are you going to have him picked up," Monica asked.

"No, not yet."

If I had him picked up now, I might never find out what he is up to. Until I know just what was going on, I was unsure of what I could do about it.

Suddenly, the phone rang again. I reached over and picked it up.

"Hello."

"Mr. McCord, this is Mr. Bradford's secretary. Is Mr. Bradford there with you?"

"Yes, just one moment," I replied.

I held the receiver out for Sam. He looked at me then took it.

I didn't really pay very much attention to what was being said on the phone, as I was too busy with my own thoughts. I was hoping that Sam would get off the phone as soon as possible. I didn't want to miss a call from Cooper.

"Nick," Sam said holding his hand over the receiver of the phone. "Boyer is in my office asking about the video tapes on Jeff. What do I tell him?"

If Boyer was in Sam's office, he had to be still looking for Jeff. If that was the case, there was little doubt in my mind that he had no idea where Jeff was at the moment. I had this feeling that Boyer would do anything to get what he wanted. I had to wonder if he was party to these phone calls.

"Sam, go to your office and show Boyer the same video tapes that you showed us, but just the first ones. Don't show him the ones where Jeff is dressed like a woman. While he is watching, I'm going to call him. I want you to observe his reaction when I tell him about the phone calls."

"Got it", he replied, then told his secretary that he would be there in a minute.

I watched as Sam left the room. I noticed that he had left a guard outside the door.

"What do you hope to prove?" Monica asked.

"I hope to find out if Boyer knows about the calls here."

"What will that prove?"

"If he knows about the calls, then we know who we are dealing with. If he doesn't, then we have another party besides Boyer to contend with."

"That would make things a little more complicated, wouldn't it?"

"Yes, it would."

Monica sat quietly in the chair and looked out the window. It was easy to see that the threat on her life worried her even though she tried to keep it from me.

I closed my eyes and let my thoughts go to Monica. Even with my eyes closed I could picture her long, blond, silky hair gently blowing in the breeze on the day that I arrived at her apartment in Madison. She was looking down at me from her balcony. The soft summer sweater and dark slacks that she wore showed off the smooth lines of her beautiful figure. And I could never forget those lovely cobalt blue eyes and how they sparkled, and how she always carried herself with confidence.

Suddenly, I realized that the threat on Monica's life had consumed my mind. I was letting my mind go off into a dreamland. I didn't need that now. What I really needed to do was clear my head and start thinking more clearly. I couldn't allow my deep concerns for Monica's safety to clutter my mind. After all, she was sitting across the room from me and there was an armed guard just outside the door. It was time for me to start thinking like a cop if I was going to have any chance of figuring out just what was going on.

I looked at my watch. If Jeff's speech had lasted as long as it was scheduled to last, he would be on his way here. I started looking for Cooper's cell phone number.

"What are you looking for?" Monica asked.

"Cooper's cell phone number."

"It's on the table, on that stationary," she reminded me.

I found it right where she said it would be. I picked up the receiver and dialed the number.

"Cooper."

"Cooper, this is Nick."

"Yeah. I was just getting ready to call you."

"Do you know where Holcome is?"

"I sure do. He's about three hundred feet in front of me on Highway 2 just about three miles west of the junction of Interstate 395."

"How far is that from Knollwoods Resort and Casino?"

"I would say maybe fifteen or twenty miles, maybe a little less."

"Great. Do you think he's coming here?"

"Sure looks like it. He left his hotel without checking out. It looks like he left just about everything he had there. He didn't leave with any luggage. He rented a car at the motel and drove away. It looks like he might be planning on going back to Hartford."

"I wouldn't count on that."

"What are you thinking?"

"If he's planning on disappearing, what better way to disappear than to just walk away from everything," I said.

"You think that's what he's doing?"

"I don't know. But if he's coming here, he has several thousand dollars waiting for him at the Two Trees Inn."

"I don't understand," Cooper replied.

"I'll explain later, but my guess is that he will go directly to Two Trees Inn. Give me his license plate number and a description of the car he is driving. If he turns into Two Trees Inn, just drive by and park at the far end of Knollwoods parking lot near the main entrance. I'll find you there."

"Okay," Cooper replied.

After I got the license plate number and a description of the car Jeff was driving, I hung up the phone. I then dialed Boyer's cell phone. I knew that if he had it with him, he would be answering it in Sam's Office. The phone rang only twice before it was answered.

"Hello?"

"Boyer?"

"Nick?"

I found it interesting that he was talking to me rather softly as if he didn't want anyone nearby to hear him. Since I knew where he was, and he didn't know where I was calling from, I had the advantage.

"Yeah."

"Can I call you back in a couple of minutes?"

"No. I need to talk to you right now."

There was a moment of silence before he responded.

"Okay, he said reluctantly. "What is it?"

"I got a couple of calls from someone who threatened to kill Monica if I didn't hand over Jeff and the disks he has."

"Do you know where Jeff is?"

The one thing I noticed in his voice was that he didn't seem to care if Monica was threatened or not. I wasn't sure if it was a case of he just didn't care, or if he already knew that she had been threatened. And if he knew, then there was a good chance that he knew who had made the calls.

"Where are you now?"

"In our room at Knollwoods Resort and Casino," I said.

I thought I could hear a slight gasp, then all I could hear was dead silence on the phone. I got the impression that he didn't know that we had returned to Knollwoods. That caught me a little off guard. If he didn't know we were here, then it was very unlikely that he knew about the threats on Monica's life.

Now I was really confused. Jeff was on his way to Knollwoods. Cooper had said that he was on his tail. So it was pretty clear that Jeff had not made the calls. Since Boyer apparently didn't know that we had returned to Knollwoods, it didn't seem logical that he would have made them. In that case, who did make the calls?

"Where are you?" I asked, knowing perfectly well where he was.

"Ah - - I'm - - I'm in Groton where you told me to stay," he replied nervously.

"Stay there until I call for you," I instructed him.

"Sure thing," he replied, then hung up.

I knew that as soon as Boyer left Sam's office, Sam would come to our room. I had no idea how long Boyer would be willing to stay in Sam's office. My best guess was that he would get out of Knollwoods as soon as possible.

I let out a long sigh as I looked over at Monica. She was looking at me, and the look on her face told me that she was more than a little concerned.

"Boyer doesn't know that we are here, does he?" Monica asked.

"No, he doesn't. Well, he didn't."

"Then who else are we dealing with?" Monica asked, her voice cracking slightly.

"Come here," I said as I held out my arms.

Monica got up and walked across the room and sat down on the bed beside me. I wrapped my arms around her and pulled her close to me. She laid her head on my shoulder. I could feel the tension in her body.

"I'm not going to let anything happen to you," I said in an effort to reassure her.

I wanted to get her out of here, send her back to Madison, but I knew that would not do any good. I had placed her in danger and there was no way out of it except to find out who it was that wanted Jeff and the disks so badly.

Time passed slowly as we waited. We waited to hear from Cooper, and we waited for Sam to come back. If there was anything that I have learned over the years, it is that waiting is often the hardest thing to do. It doesn't seem to matter what you are waiting for, good news or bad news, it just seems to take forever.

My thoughts were suddenly interrupted by a knock on my door. I walked across the room and peeked through the peephole in the door to see who was there. I could see Sam standing in front of the door. I reached down and opened the door to let him in.

"Well, what do you think," Sam asked as he stepped into the room.

"I don't think he made the calls," I said as I turned and walked back into the room to join Monica.

"I don't think so either. He really got nervous while talking to you. What did you say to him?"

"I told him I was here. I think he was of the impression we were still in Hartford or that we had returned to Chicago. I don't think he knew that we had returned here."

"Well, he left as soon as you hung up."

"He didn't stay to see the videos?"

"No. He said that he had to go. That he would have to look at them later."

"I wonder what his hurry was?" Monica asked.

"I don't know, but I may have spilled the beans when I told him about the threat on your life," I said.

"How's that?" Sam asked.

"Now he knows that there's someone else out there who is interested in getting their hands on Jeff's disks. I doubt very seriously that Boyer likes the competition."

"You are probably right about that," Sam agreed.

"What's our next step?" Monica asked.

"We wait and see what Jeff does next. I doubt that we will have to wait very long. I think things will happen pretty fast once Jeff gets back here."

"What do we need to do to get ready?" Sam asked.

"Get some of your people ready to close in on Jeff's room at Two Trees Inn, and get a couple of extra guards up here. I want to know everything that goes on at Two Trees Inn. Anything that is the least bit out of the ordinary."

"You got it," Sam replied.

I again sat down next to Monica and put my arm around her. She leaned over against me and listened to Sam as he gave instructions to his people on what he wanted them to do. He also placed a call to the tribal police for back up.

Now we were as ready as we could be. We had no idea what was going to happen next, but we had done all we could to prepare for it. Now it was time to just sit and wait.

CHAPTER FOURTEEN

Monica and I sat on the edge of the bed while Sam sat in one of the chairs at the small table. While we waited for a call from Cooper, I kept trying to think of where Jeff might go if he didn't come back to Knollwoods Resort and Casino or Two Trees Inn. No matter how hard I tried, I could not think of any other place that he might go. There just seemed to be too much waiting for him here, namely well over five thousand dollars in cash and Miss Marshall. I was hoping that I was right, but what if I wasn't? If I wasn't right I could easily lose track of Jeff and never find him again, or I would find him dead.

Just then the phone began to ring. I leaned over to the bedside stand and grabbed the receiver.

"Hello?"

"This Nick?"

"Yeah."

"This is Cooper."

"Where are you?" I asked."

"I'm just outside of Norwick. Your friend just stopped at a small motel here on the edge of town."

"He did what?"

"He stopped at a motel. After going into the office, he came out and went to a room near the back, away from the street."

"He checked into a motel?" I asked, finding it hard to believe that he had stopped at a motel.

"Yes, he has."

"You got any ideas what he is doing there?"

"No. None at all. After he went to his room, I checked with the desk clerk in the office. It seems that he checked in and paid for two nights, in cash."

"That's interesting. Say, what name did he use?"

"He checked in as William Grant."

"That's the same name that he used to check into the Two Trees Inn here. Janet Marshall is staying in his room here. She's listed as Mrs. Grant."

"What are these two up to?" Cooper asked.

"I don't know, but you stay on Jeff. I don't want to lose him. I have Miss Marshall under surveillance here."

"Got it. Hey, wait a second," Cooper said just as I was about to hang up.

"Yeah? What's up? Is he on the move again?"

"No. A woman just came out of the room Jeff just checked into. That's strange. There was no woman with him when he got here. He was alone in the car."

"Maybe she was waiting for him?" I suggested.

"I don't think so. There's something strange going on here," Cooper said.

"What makes you think the woman wasn't waiting for him?"

"When I checked with the desk clerk, he said that Jeff didn't have reservations. He just stopped in and asked for a room that was away from the street. If that was the case, he wasn't expecting a woman to be in his room. It might be a good idea if I check his room and see if he is still there."

My mind was trying to decipher all that had been going on. Then it hit me. Jeff was using the motel as a place to change clothes, but where did he get the clothes? Cooper had said that he left Hartford without any luggage.

"Cooper, don't go near that room. You said that Jeff left Hartford without his luggage. Did he have anything with him? Maybe, his computer case or a brief case?"

"Yeah. Now that you mention it, he had his computer case with him, but no other luggage. You know, that black one that he always carries and never lets out of his sight."

"Does the woman have a black computer case?"

"Yeah."

"Follow the woman. And whatever you do, don't lose her," I said practically yelling in the phone.

"What? I thought you wanted me to keep an eye on Jeff?"

I could hear the confusion in Cooper's voice. He must have thought that I had gone over the edge.

"I do. That woman is Jeff. Follow him and don't let him out of your sight. My bet is he will be coming here."

"Okay, if you say so. She, ah, he's getting back in the car. I have to go."

Just then the phone went dead. I looked over at Sam. I could tell by the look on his face that he was wondering what was going on. I took a minute to explain.

"Do you think he is coming back here dressed as a woman?"

"Yes. I do. Why not? It worked for him before. Everyone is looking for a man. What better way to hide than to be a woman when everyone is looking for a man?"

"I see your point. What do we do now?"

"I think we should drive to the end of the parking lot and wait there. It will put us just across the street from Two Trees Inn," I suggested. "I would like to be close just in case things start to happen.

"Good idea," Sam replied.

"Can calls to this phone be transferred to your car? I don't want to miss a call from Cooper."

"Sure. I'll have that done," Sam said as he picked up the phone and called his office.

Jeff was playing this very cool. He probably knew that everyone would be looking for a man. This way if the Two

Trees Inn was being watched, he could walk right into the Two Trees Inn and no one would realize he was there.

We left the hotel and drove to the far end of the parking lot in Sam's big Cadillac sedan. From where we were parked we could see the entrance to the Two Trees Inn parking lot. We could not see much else as the lot was surrounded with large, thick pine trees. At least we would be able to see Jeff when he arrived. He would have to drive right past us.

It was quiet in the car as we sat waiting. My mind turned back to the phone call that I had received earlier. I was trying to think, to clear my mind of everything except the voice that I had heard on the phone. I knew that I had heard that voice before. If I could figure out who it was that had called me, I might be able to figure out who else was involved in all this.

Suddenly, it came to me where I had heard that voice before. It was the voice of one of Sam Bradford's own security people. I looked at Sam. He was sitting behind the wheel of his car looking out the windshield toward the inn. He looked as if he was deep in thought.

I wasn't sure what I should do. I found it difficult to believe that Sam would be double-crossing me. What reason would he have? After all, he had been very cooperative and open with me almost from the very beginning. He didn't seem to be hiding anything. If he had wanted Jeff, he could have had him at almost anytime. He knew where Jeff was most of the time while he was here. It didn't seem to make sense to me that he was involved in anything criminal.

My gut feeling told me that Sam didn't know that one of his security people had been bought. If he did know, it would not be good for that individual.

"What are you thinking?" Monica asked me.

Monica's voice broke the silence that had consumed the car. Sam turned and looked over his shoulder at her. From the look on his face, he was not sure what she had said.

"Sam?"

"Yeah," he replied as he turned back and looked at me.

"I think I know whose voice that was on the phone."

"Whose?"

"One of your security people," I said as I watched and waited to see Sam's reaction.

"What?" he said, his voice showing his disbelief.

"One of your security people was the one that called me."

"Are you sure?"

"Yes."

"Which one?" Sam demanded to know.

"I don't know what his name is, but it's the one that came to our room with you the first time we talked. When we got to your office, he stopped and talked to your secretary while we went on into your office. That was where I heard his voice before. It was in your office."

"That would be Richard Rossburg."

"Where is he supposed to be now?"

"I don't know. I'll have to call my office and find out."

"Be careful what you say. We don't want him to know that we are wise to him. I don't want him to run," I said.

"If he is in on this, he will wish he wasn't," Sam said, his voice showing his anger at one of his people being on the take.

Sam reached out and picked up the car phone. He called his office.

Monica and I watched and listened as he talked on the phone. I hoped that he didn't say anything that would give the person on the other end any idea that there might be something wrong. Sam did a very good job of keeping his anger out of his voice.

"Rossburg is off duty at the moment," Sam said as he hung up the phone. My guess is that he has gone home."

"This confuses the situation some. If he's involved we may have problems."

"Yeah, I'm sure you're right," Sam agreed.

"Maybe you could reduce the problem if you could get Rossburg to come to your office and then keep him there until we know what is going on with Jeff," Monica suggested.

I looked from Monica to Sam. There was no doubt in my mind that what she suggested was a good idea. The only problem I could see with it was that there was no telling how long we would have to keep him out of the picture. We still didn't know what Jeff was planning on doing, or how long it would take for us to find out.

"That's not a bad idea, but. . . ,"

The ringing of the car phone suddenly interrupted me. Sam reached over and picked up the phone.

"This is Bradford," he said.

Monica and I listened, but we could only hear one side of the conversation. The more Sam talked the more worried he looked. I had to wonder what was going on.

"What?"

Sam now seemed to be getting upset, even angry again. Monica looked at me. The look on her face told me that she was as interested as I was to know what was being said.

"NO! Don't do anything. Just keep an eye on Miss Marshall," he said sharply.

"We've got a problem," Sam said as he hung up the phone.

"What's wrong," Monica asked before I had a chance.

"The two men I have watching Miss Marshall called to check and see if I had put a second car on watch. They told me that a second car drove into the parking lot about ten minutes ago, but no one got out."

"Any idea who they might be?" I asked.

"Bill Simpson, one of my men watching Miss Marshall, got interested in the car and snuck over behind it. He was able to get close enough to identify one of the men sitting in the car. It was Rossburg. It seems that Rossburg and someone Bill couldn't recognize have staked out Miss Marshall's room, too," Sam explained.

"He's not supposed to be there, is he?"

"No."

"Damn," I said as I began to think about what problems it might cause.

That was all we needed, more people in the way. But if Rossburg was involved, then we had two groups of people that were looking for Jeff. We had suspected for some time that there were two people, but this clinched it. At least now we knew who the other one was, or should I say, we now knew who was representing the other one.

This made things more difficult. We knew that Boyer was after the game disks, and now we had a pretty good idea that Rossburg was after them, too. What we didn't know was who was representing who?

"I think we need to eliminate Rossburg from the picture," Sam said.

I looked at Monica, than back at Sam. I wasn't real sure what he meant by "eliminate", but I had to agree that we needed to get Rossburg out of the way.

"You're not going to - - ?" Monica asked.

"No. No, we just want him out of the way," Sam reassured Monica. "If Boyer and Rossburg clash in an effort to get the disks, I'm convinced that someone will get hurt and it could be Miss Marshall," he said.

"I have to agree," I said. "We need to take Rossburg out, and I think we need to do it now, before Jeff gets here. Once Jeff is here, it will be far more difficult and a lot more risky."

"I'll check with my men on watch and see if anyone else is around that we have to worry about," Sam said.

"Good idea," I said.

As Sam got on the car phone again, I began to try and think of a way that we could get Rossburg and his partner out of the picture without disturbing our setup. It had to be done before Boyer and his people found out about Miss Marshall and where she was staying. It also had to be done before Jeff showed up.

"Nick?"

"Yeah, honey."

"How are you going to get close to these men without being seen?"

"I haven't figured that out yet."

"Nick, do you have a gun?" Sam asked.

"No."

Sam reached over and opened the glove box. He reached in and pulled out a .38 caliber pistol and handed it to me. I checked it, then slipped it into my belt.

"We best get going before Jeff shows up," Sam said.

"Yeah," I replied as I opened the car door.

"I'm going with you," Monica said as a matter of fact, then opened the car door and got out.

"I don't think it's a good idea," Sam replied.

I didn't think it was a good idea either, but I knew Monica well enough to know that she would not be left behind. Besides, I would rather have her with me and know where she was than to have her suddenly appear in the middle of things as someone's hostage.

"I don't think we have a choice," I said to Sam as I got out of the car.

Sam didn't say anything more, but I could see by the look on his face that he was not very happy about her coming along. He simply got out of the car and walked around to join us.

We walked across the street and up the grassy embankment to the trees. With all the trees between the inn and us, it was easy for us to move closer to the parking lot without being seen. In the darkness of night and the thickness of the trees that surrounded the parking lot, we could have snuck up on just about anyone.

We worked our way through the trees until we could see into the parking lot. Sam pointed out where his people were hiding so that they could keep an eye on Miss Marshall's room as well as see everyone who came in or left the inn's parking lot. It was easy to see why no one would know they were there. The rows of thick pine trees provided excellent cover.

He also pointed out where his people were that were waiting in the car. They were well hidden back in the corner of the parking lot, yet they were ready to move at a moment's notice, if need be.

Sam then pointed out the car that Rossburg was in. I took a minute to look around. It was not going to be easy to get to them. Their car was parked between two other cars and there were two rows of cars parked behind them. Except for the cover that the other cars would provide, it was open space.

"It's going to be hard to get close to them without being seen," I whispered to Sam. "There's just too much open space."

"If we could get behind the car that is parked directly behind them, we could rush them," Sam suggested.

"No. If we come up right behind them, they might see us in their rearview mirrors. If they see us, it could cause a commotion and give us away to anyone else that might be around. We would lose the element of surprise and it could get someone hurt," I said.

"You're probably right. What do you suggest?"

"If we could get behind the two cars on either side of them, it would put us at least a full car length closer to them. If we rush them from there, we might be able to get the drop on them before they realize what is happening," I suggested as an option.

"Nick," Monica whispered as she reached out and touched my arm.

"What is it, honey?"

"If you had something to distract them, wouldn't it make it easier and less risky?"

"Sure. What do you have in mind?"

"If the two of you got into position, then I could walk into the parking lot from near the entrance and walk along the front of the inn, right past the room Miss Marshall is in."

"They would be watching her to see if she stops at Miss Marshall's room," Sam said as he began to grasp her plan. "Sounds like a good idea to me."

"Rossburg knows you," I reminded Monica.

"But I don't think he would be able to recognize me if I keep the lights behind me and don't look out toward the parking lot."

I was reluctant to let her do it, but if it gave us just a few seconds more it might work.

"Are you sure you want to do this?" I asked.

"Yes," she replied looking into my eyes.

"Okay, but as soon as we have Rossburg and his partner, I want you to get out of there. Duck around the corner and wait for us. Both Jeff and Miss Marshall know you. If they see you, we could lose Jeff. He won't stick around if he thinks we are on to him."

"I understand," Monica said.

"We better get started before Jeff shows up," Sam said as a reminder of how short a time we had.

"Be careful," I whispered to Monica, then leaned over to her and kissed her lightly on the lips.

"I will," she replied, then turned and disappeared in among the trees.

As I watched Monica disappear into the darkness, I began to think of what I had gotten her into. Even if it was her idea for her to be a decoy, it was not entirely to my liking. Yet, I could see no other way for us to get to Rossburg and his partner without losing the element of surprise. That didn't make me like the situation any better.

“Nick, you take the passenger side, I’ll take Rossburg,” Sam whispered interrupting my thoughts.

“Okay, but let’s try to do this as quickly and quietly as we can,” I whispered. “If you have to cold-cock Rossburg to keep him quiet, do it.”

“Got yah,” he replied.

I nodded that I was ready so I moved along the row of trees until I was where I could work my way toward our target. As I started to move out into the parking lot, I caught a glimpse of Sam as he crouched down and moved up behind a car. I crouched down and began to move from car to car, making sure that Rossburg or his partner could not see me.

The going was slow as I moved closer and closer to our target. It took me awhile to get to my position behind the car just to the right of the car that Rossburg and his partner were in.

As I leaned against the back of the car, I again checked my gun to make sure it was ready. I was hoping that I would not have to use it, but I had to be ready for anything.

It was only a matter of seconds before Sam was kneeling down behind the car on the other side of Rossburg’s car. We took a minute to silently let each other know that we were ready. Now it was time to wait for Monica to distract them.

“Hey, who’s that?” I heard one of the men in the car say.

Whoever said it did not know that he had given us our clue to attack. That one little comment was all we needed to know that their attention was on Monica.

I nodded at Sam, then jumped up and ran up next to the car. I reached in the open window and grabbed the man by the collar and stuck the barrel of my gun against the side of his head. He instantly froze.

“One sound and it will be your last,” I said softly, yet firmly. I decided to let the gun do most of my talking.

When the man didn’t move, I looked across the car and saw that Sam had Rossburg. He had his gun in Rossburg’s face.

"Okay, gentlemen, very slowly put your hands on top of your heads and interlace your fingers," I said as I carefully pulled my gun back away from the man's head.

As soon as they had done what I told them, I put the barrel of my gun under the man's chin and pushed his head back against the headrest. With my free hand, I reached inside the car and under his coat. I removed his gun from his shoulder holster and tucked it in my belt. Then I watched as Sam did the same thing to Rossburg.

"Keep your hands on top of your head and very slowly get out of the car," I ordered as I took a step back and opened the car door.

The man slowly turned and swung his feet out of the car. As he leaned forward to standup, I reached up with my free hand and grabbed his hands on top of his head from behind him. By pinching his fingers together, I reduced his ability to get aggressive.

"Not a sound," I reminded them.

I now had my man under control. With his hands pinched together and my gun in his back, I could lead him anywhere. I looked over to the other side of the car and saw Sam making Rossburg do the same thing I had made Rossburg's partner do.

I started walking my prisoner toward the back of the parking lot. I wanted him out of sight just in case Jeff showed up. Sam was right behind me with Rossburg. I had noticed that Sam was not too gentle with him, but I couldn't blame him for that. I would not have been very happy with someone like that, either.

Once we got our prisoners back in the trees, we were greeted by a couple of tribal policemen. They quickly cuffed Rossburg and his partner. It was then that I recognized the man I had captured.

"I know you," I said to him.

"You don't know nothing," he spat back angrily.

"Who is he, Nick?" Sam asked.

"He was one of the men that met Boyer at the airport."

"You mean he works for Boyer?"

"Worked for Boyer would be a better way to put it," I said.

"I don't work for no one," he snapped. When my lawyer gets done with you, you'll wish you never saw me."

"If I were you, I wouldn't give a damn about my lawyer. But I'd be just a little worried about Boyer when he finds out that you double-crossed him. I've seen his rap sheet. I seriously doubt that your life would be worth a nickel," I said quietly and in a matter of fact tone.

The expression on the guy's face changed from one of defiance to one filled with fear. He apparently hadn't given much thought to what Boyer was capable of doing to someone who would double-cross him. It seemed that he was suddenly thinking about it and from the look on his face he didn't like what came to mind.

"Take them to my office and keep them there. Don't let them out of your sight, and don't let anyone talk to them," Sam ordered.

"You can't do this. I have rights," Rossburg insisted.

"If he opens his mouth one more time, close it."

"Yes, sir," one of the guards replied with a grin.

Sam and I stood at the edge of the trees and watched as the two were led off across the road to a waiting tribal police car. I was glad that part was over.

"We better get Monica out of there before Jeff gets here," I said as I turned and started back into the trees.

Sam followed me back toward the parking lot. When we came out of the trees, I looked toward the inn. There was no one around. I couldn't see Monica anywhere.

"Where did Monica go?" I asked as Sam stepped up beside me.

"I don't know," he replied as he looked around.

"If she went where I told her she should be just around that corner," I said as I pointed toward the building.

"Let's check with my men. She's probably just waiting around the corner, but let's check."

I nodded that I agreed. I followed him along the edge of the trees where we were not likely to be seen. When we got to the corner where two of his men were parked while they watched the inn, we crouched down and moved up along side the car.

"You guys see where that blond went?" Sam asked.

"The one walking in front of the inn?"

"Yeah,"

"She went around the end of the building."

"Thanks. Keep an eye out. We expect Holcome at any time, but he may be dressed as a woman."

"Yes, sir."

Sam turned and motioned for me to go back into the trees. Once hidden in the trees, we started working our way around the edge of the parking lot toward the end of the building.

Once we got close enough to the building, I could see Monica standing next to the wall several feet back from the corner. She was almost hidden in the shadows. She seemed glad to see us when we stepped out of the trees.

"Did you get them?" she asked in a whisper.

"We sure did. I don't know how much we will get out of them, but we got them out of our way," I said.

"Thanks for helping," Sam said.

Monica smiled at Sam, then looked at me. It was clear that she was glad that she could be of help. I think I even noticed a little spark of pride in the sparkle of her beautiful blue eyes. It was like she was glad that she was able to do her part in this investigation, not that she hadn't already done her part.

"I'm proud of you," I whispered in her ear.

"Thanks," she whispered back.

"What now, Nick," Sam asked.

"I guess we wait for Jeff to show, but I think we need to find a better place."

I walked to the corner of the building and looked down along the wall. It was three doors, or rooms, down the wall to the room that Miss Marshall was in. Looking around, it became clear that this was as close as we were going to get. I had hoped for something better.

"How about over there," Sam whispered as he pointed to a small cluster of trees and bushes in the parking lot that would put us only a few feet closer to the door to Miss Marshall's room, but almost directly in front of it.

I looked first to the cluster of trees, then at the door to the room. There was no doubt that it was a few feet closer than we had been and there was a little less cover, but it did give us a better view of anyone who might approach the room. It might also give us a chance to see into the room if the door was opened. We would have to stay low and up close to the bushes or anyone coming by would be able to see us.

"It doesn't have the greatest cover, but it's better than what we have here. Let's go down behind those cars and come up from behind it," I instructed.

"Okay."

Sam wasted no time. He moved out and ducked down behind a car. We watched him as he worked his way from one car to the next until he was behind the bushes. Once he was in place, Monica and I followed.

Before long, we joined Sam behind the cluster of trees and bushes. We settled in to wait and watch. A quick check of my watch assured me that we would not have long to wait.

CHAPTER FIFTEEN

We didn't have to wait long before a car came around the end of the row of trees and into the parking lot. It moved along very slowly through the parking lot. It was the car that Cooper had described to me over the phone.

As it passed by a light, I could see what appeared to be a woman driving the car. She looked as if she might be looking for someone. I could also see that she was looking between the rows of cars and at each car as she passed by. I got a good look at the woman in the car as it slowly rolled by our hiding place. I could see that the woman was not a woman.

The person in the car was Jeff, and it quickly became obvious to me that he was trying to make sure that he was not driving into a trap. The fact that he was being very cautious simply reinforced my belief that he knew what was going on, which was considerably more than I knew.

"What do you think he's up to?" Sam asked in a whisper.

"He's trying to make sure that no one is around. I hope he doesn't see your men in the car," I replied softly as I ducked down to avoid having the headlights of the car shine on me.

As soon as Jeff had finished his drive around the parking lot, he stopped in front of the door to the room where Miss Marshall was staying. The parking spaces in front of the room were occupied. I could see him looking around for a place to park that was close to the room. The closest parking space was several cars down from the door. Jeff drove down to the open parking space, stopped and looked around.

"What's he doing?" Monica asked in a whisper.

"He's trying to decide if he should park or leave. Maybe he's waiting to see if a space opens up closer to his room. I'm sure he doesn't want to park too far away from the room. He probably wants to be able to get out of here in a hurry if something goes wrong."

I continued to watch him. It seemed to take him a long time before he decided that it was safe for him to park in the open space. When he finally decided to park, he backed his car into the parking space, then sat there looking around. He was being very careful, but then I couldn't blame him. He had some pretty tough and savvy people hunting for him, and from his actions I was sure he knew it.

It seemed like it took forever before I noticed the dome light come on in his car. That meant that he had opened the door and was going to get out of the car.

Suddenly, I saw a big car turn into the parking lot from the street. It looked like a Lincoln Town Car. I noticed that Jeff quickly shut the car door, which turned off the dome light. I could see him duck down low in the car so that he could not be seen.

My attention quickly turned to the Lincoln Town Car. It moved slowly along the front of the inn. I could see the driver looking at the doors of the inn. The car came to a stop in front of the room that Miss Marshall was in.

Just as the doors on the car opened, I saw another vehicle pull into the parking lot and stop at the entrance. It was a Chevy Tahoe and it was blocking the entrance to the parking lot. My guess was that it was there to prevent anyone from leaving.

"I think we have a problem," I whispered as I glanced over at Sam.

"Yeah. I see it. What do you want to do?" Sam asked.

"Get your men to close in on that Chevy Tahoe at the entrance to the parking lot. And have your guys in the car ready to move at any indication that Jeff is going to make a run for it."

Sam nodded that he understood and immediately got on his two-way radio. He gave his men their instructions as quietly as possible. When he finished, he looked at me and nodded that his men were ready for anything.

I watched as a man got out of the Lincoln Town Car. He stood beside the car and looked around the parking lot for a moment or two. It was none other than Kenneth Boyer and he was checking out the area before the other man got out.

After a moment or so, Boyer bent down and said something to the man inside. The back door of the car opened and the other man got out.

I didn't recognize the one that got out of the back seat, but it appeared to me that Boyer was working for him. The driver remained in the car and stayed behind the wheel with the motor still running.

The man with Boyer was well dressed and he looked like he might be someone of some importance. Boyer seemed to be looking to him for instructions, which gave me the impression that this man might very well be in charge.

After they looked around and seemed satisfied that it was clear, the man motioned for Boyer to move around to the other side of the car.

They walked up to the door to Miss Marshall's room, then stood there a moment or two looking around. It was clear to me that they were trying to make sure that no one was watching them.

From my position, I could see the front door of the room clearly. Boyer reached out and knocked on the door. I couldn't see his hands, but from his movements I was sure that he had reached inside his coat. His actions convinced me that he was reaching for a gun.

Suddenly, the door opened. I could see the smile on Miss Marshall's face quickly turn to one of shock. Her jaw dropped and her eyes got big. I also noticed her eyes dropped down as she started to slowly back away as if Boyer had a gun pointed at her, which I'm sure he did.

Boyer stepped into the room while the other man looked toward the Chevy Tahoe at the end of the parking lot. He then stepped into the room and closed the door.

Time had come for us to move. I needed the men in the Chevy Tahoe at the entrance to the parking lot taken out. I also needed to get Jeff before he blew the whole thing by trying to run.

"Sam, have your men take out the guys at the entrance. I want it done quickly and quietly. And tell them to just take over the vehicle, but don't move it."

"You got it," he said, then got on his radio to give his men their instructions.

"What about Jeff?" Monica asked in a whisper.

"I want you and Sam to get him. He doesn't know Sam. Monica, you keep your face hidden from him. If he sees you, he might try to run. Just walk over there as if the two of you had been necking in a car. You know, straighten your blouse and laugh like you have been having a good time. As you pass by his car, Sam, you take him. And be careful. We don't know if he has a gun or not."

"Did you get that?" Monica asked Sam.

"Yeah. Nick, my guys are ready."

"Okay," I said as I took a deep breath. "As soon as you can see your guys moving in, start for Jeff. Hopefully, he will be watching what is going on at the entrance and you will be able to get close to him before he knows what is happening."

"What about you?"

"I'm going to get the driver in the Lincoln," I replied. "Let's go."

Sam immediately gave the command for his men to move in. Monica pulled her blouse loose from her slacks. With Sam's arm around her waist, they began walking across the parking lot toward Jeff.

I quickly ducked down and moved from one car to the next covering the ground between the driver and me as fast as I could. As I got close, I could see the driver's attention was on the door to Miss Marshall's room. If he would keep it there long enough for me to get within reach of him, I could take him out of the picture.

I crouched down and moved quietly along side the Lincoln until I was close to the driver's door. I then jumped up in front of him and pointed my gun in his face. The look on his face was priceless. It was one of total surprise and shock.

"You may be able to warn them that I'm here, but you won't live long enough to find out if it did any good. You want to die right here?" I asked softly, but with as much conviction in my voice as possible.

The man just sat there not moving a muscle. He was petrified with the fear that he was going to die.

"Get out very quietly," I said as I reached out, pulled on the door handle and opened the car door.

As soon as he was out of the vehicle, I had him put his hands on his head and I walked him around to the other side of the car. A quick pat down revealed that he was not carrying a gun. That indicated to me that he was just a driver, nothing more.

"Nick, over here."

I immediately recognized Sam's voice, and turned to see where he was. He was crouched down next to a car. He had a gun in his hand. There was a tribal policeman with him. I could not see anyone else, but I was sure that he had Monica and Jeff nearby and safely hidden.

I turned my prisoner toward Sam and sort of pushed him in that direction. As soon as he was in the custody of Sam, I turned my attention back to the door to Miss Marshall's room.

I moved up against the wall between the window and the door to Miss Marshall's room. From there I could hear voices inside.

"All I want from you is to know where Holcome is. I don't want to have to hurt you."

"I don't know where he is," Miss Marshall cried.

I didn't recognize the voice so I was sure it was not Boyer's. The only thing I could tell from what I could hear was that Miss Marshall was scared to death, but that was certainly understandable.

"When is he supposed to get here?"

"Answer him," Boyer said in a threatening tone.

I thought I could hear Miss Marshall moan in pain. That convinced me that Boyer was putting a little muscle behind the questions.

"I don't know," she cried again.

"Where are his disks?" the voice demanded.

"I don't know. I don't know. Please don't hurt me."

I had heard about all I wanted. I now knew what they were after, and that they were willing to do almost anything to get them. It was time to interfere with their plans.

I took a look around. Sam was crouched down behind a car, his gun in his hand. He was ready. That gave me reason to believe that his men were ready, too.

I motioned for him to have someone get the Lincoln out from in front of the room. Almost immediately one of Sam's men came out of hiding, moved around to the driver's side of the car, slipped inside and quietly moved it out of the way. We were now ready.

"Okay, Boyer. You and your friend had best come out with your hands in the air," I said as I prepared myself for almost anything.

There was dead silence. It didn't take a genius to figure out that we had caught them off guard. It had to have passed through their minds that we had already taken out their backup.

"Is that you, Nick?" Boyer asked.

I could hear a faint tone of amusement in his voice.

"Yeah, it's me."

"I'll give you credit for sticking to it, but you can't pull this off alone."

"What makes you think that I'm alone?"

"Oh, I forgot. You have a partner, and just what is she going to do?"

"Come on out with your hands up," I insisted, not wanting to carry on a long discussion with him.

"We have Miss Marshall in here," Boyer said.

It didn't take much to figure out what he meant. He planned to use her as a shield.

"Sorry, Boyer. It won't work. I have the tribal police out here. They have your men at the entrance in custody and they're not about to let you out of here. You might as well give it up."

I could hear voices inside, but I couldn't make out what was being said. If I had to guess, I would have said that Boyer and his boss were discussing what to do next. Knowing a little about Boyer from police reports, I felt he might give it up without a fight. After all, he had gotten out of worse jams than this in the past. All we had against him at the moment was threatening a person with a gun and assault. It was the other man that concerned me. I knew nothing about him.

"I'm coming out," Boyer said, the tone of his voice indicating that he knew that he would be able to get out of this without much difficulty.

"Okay. Come out with your hands on top of your head and walk straight out into the parking lot."

"Okay, I'm coming."

I turned toward the door and leaned back against the wall. As the door slowly opened, I readied myself just in case he decided that he would attack me instead.

Boyer stepped into the doorway with his hands above his head, then took one or two steps forward when a shot rang out from inside the room. A look of surprise and pain quickly showed on Boyer's face as he reached for his back.

He staggered forward and started to fall as the door behind him slammed shut.

Boyer fell face down on the ground and didn't move. Everything happened so fast that no one had time to react. As for me, I pressed myself up against the wall as tight as I could and hoped that no one returned fire. I didn't like the idea of being in the middle of a gunfight, literally. Luckily, Sam's men were well trained. They didn't return fire, but kept their positions and remained ready.

"Who's out there?" the man in the room asked.

"It's me, Mr. Conway. Sam Bradford."

I looked at Sam. It came as a bit of a surprise that Sam knew who this man was.

"What are you doing here?"

"You know darn well why I'm here. You can't commit crimes on tribal land without having to deal with me."

I wondered what Sam was getting at. As far as I knew he was the Chief of Security at Knollwoods Resort and Casino, and nothing more.

"You're going to let me go or I will have to kill this woman," Conway threatened.

"You know I can't let you go. You weren't wanted for anything as far as I know until you shot Boyer in the back. Oh, maybe threatening someone with a gun and possibly assault, but nothing more serious than that. Now I want you for murder."

"I'll come out when you have my car in front of this room with my driver and ready to go."

"Can't do that and you know it."

Suddenly, all hell broke loose. A shot was fired. I couldn't tell where it came from. Then without warning, Jeff came running out from behind a car. He had a gun in his hand and he was charging toward the motel room door as fast as he could run.

As he came toward me, he was pointing the gun at me and began pulling the trigger. He fired only two shots in my direction as I dove for the ground just in time for the bullets to fly by me and slam into the wall. I didn't have time to return fire. I was too busy ducking.

Jeff ran by me and slammed into the door, breaking it open. Several shots were fired inside the room. By the time I could get up, it was all over. It had lasted but a couple of seconds, but it was a hectic few seconds.

No one moved for several minutes. When I didn't hear anything, I stood up and leaned against the wall. I listened, but the only thing I could hear was the soft sobs of a woman crying.

I glanced back toward the parking lot and saw Sam looking toward me. I motioned for him to stay where he was. He crouched back down.

I turned my attention on the room. Leaning toward the door, I moved closer until I could see inside the room. The first thing I saw was this man Sam referred to as Conway sitting on the floor with his back against the wall. His hands were lying limp at his sides, and his gun was lying on the floor a couple of feet from him. His eyes were staring off into space and the front of his shirt was soaked with blood. There was no doubt in my mind that he was dead.

I turned and stepped into the room, my gun ready. I found Jeff lying on the floor. Miss Marshall was sitting on the floor and was holding his head in her lap as she rocked back and forth. Slowly her eyes looked up at me. Her eyes were pleading for me to help her, but there was little I could do.

I knelt down on the floor beside Jeff. He was still breathing, but I knew that he would probably not last more than a few minutes.

"Jeff," I said softly.

Jeff opened his eyes and looked up at me. His eyes were filled with pain. I knew that I would have just a few minutes to find out what he had planned.

"Jeff, tell me what's on the disks?"

"A game," he whispered.

"What kind of game?"

"Card game, Blackjack," he said, then coughed.

"What did Tilman and Whitman have to do with all this?"

"The three of us were going to sell the game to a German firm, but they double-crossed me."

"How?"

"They tried to - - - take it from me - - - and sell it - - - themselves. They tried to - - - cut me out," he replied weakly.

"Did you kill them?"

"Yes," he replied, then coughed again as he tried to catch his breath. "They were trying - - - to double-cross me."

"Were you trying to deal with Conway?"

"No. He was trying to - - steal the game from me. Boyer worked for Conway," he said then paused briefly before going on.

"Conway approached me - - in Chicago, but I wouldn't - - sell it to him. We already had a deal - - but he hired - - -."

Jeff closed his eyes and took a couple of rather shallow breaths. As he did, I looked up to find Sam and Monica standing behind Miss Marshall. They were all looking down at me as I questioned Jeff.

"There's an ambulance on the way," Sam said.

I turned my attention back to Jeff as he grabbed my arm.

"When I wouldn't - - sell to Conway, he hired - - Boyer to follow me - - to get the disks for him."

"Jeff, were you planning on running away with Miss Marshall?"

"Yes," he replied softly. "I love her."

I heard Miss Marshall sobbing. I couldn't help but turn my head and glance at her, but I quickly turned my attention back to Jeff.

Jeff's eyes turned away from me and he looked at Miss Marshall. A slight smile came over his face as he looked at her.

"I love you," he said in a raspy whisper, then he collapsed in her arms.

I pressed my fingers alongside his neck in the hope of finding a pulse, but there was no pulse. He was gone. The search for Jeff Holcome was over.

Monica reached down and took Miss Marshall by the shoulders. She gently helped her to her feet, than turned her away and led her out of the room.

I could hear the sound of the ambulance as it came closer and closer. It seemed a little ironic, but it was too late to help anyone here.

I stepped outside of the room and looked for Monica. She was helping Miss Marshall into one of the tribal police cars.

I saw Cooper standing to one side. He was looking at me. I walked over to him.

"I guess our job is done here," he said.

"Yeah. We found Jeff for all the good it did. I guess you will get the disks back to Games Unlimited?"

"I'll get them from Bradford and send them back. What are you going to do?"

"We'll return to Madison in a day or two."

"I can't say I liked the way I was treated in the restroom, but I certainly understand it," Cooper said with a smile.

"I'm sorry that I had to be so hard on you. You're a good man, Cooper. Thanks for all your help," I said as I stuck my hand out. "I'll see to it that you get paid for your time and effort."

"Thanks. If you ever need me again, just call," Cooper replied as he took hold of my hand.

"I will, and thanks again," I replied as we shook hands.

I let go of his hand, turned and walked toward the car where Monica was waiting. She looked tired. I was sure that with everything that had happened, she was exhausted. I know I was.

"Are we done here?" she asked as I stepped up to her.

"Yes. It's all in Sam's hands now. We have done what we came here to do, find Jeff. It's up to Sam to sort it all out and press charges against whoever is alive to charge.

"That's it?"

"Yeah. That's it.

"What do we do now?" Monica asked.

"Go back to the hotel, I guess. I can get a car to take us back to Knollwoods, if you want," I said.

"It's not very far, do you think we could walk?"

"Sure."

I reached out and put my hand in the small of her back as we started to walk across the parking lot. Monica slipped her arm around me and moved closer.

"Monica, where did Jeff get the gun?"

"He grabbed it away from one of the policemen who was supposed to be watching him. The policeman was distracted when Boyer was shot."

With our arms around each other, we walked across the street then along the street that led to Knollwoods Resort and Casino. For part of the way, we didn't say anything. I don't know what Monica was thinking about, but I was thinking about what I was going to tell Sharon.

"Nick?"

"Yeah."

"Will we have to stay here for awhile, at least until Sam gets this all sorted out?"

"I don't think so. We might have to stay for a day or two, but Sam shouldn't need us around any longer than that."

"What about those men they took back to Knollwoods and are holding until Sam gets there."

"You know, I almost forgot about them. My guess is that Sam will question them. At this point, I think the only thing that they can be charged with would be interfering in an investigation. I'm sure that Sam will figure something out.

"What about Sharon? What do you plan to tell her?"

"I see nothing can be gained by lying to her. I'll tell her everything. She has a right to know."

"Are you going to tell her that Jeff was in love with Miss Marshall?"

"Maybe not. I don't think that's important now."

Monica gave me a gentle squeeze. I was sure that she didn't want me to tell Sharon what Jeff's last words were.

We continued our walk in silence. It didn't take us very long to walk the half mile or so back to the hotel at Knollwoods.

We went directly to our room. I had one last chore to do, one that I wished I didn't have to do. I sat down on the edge of the bed and picked up the phone. After dialing Sharon's number, I waited for her to answer. Monica sat down beside me and rested her hand on my leg.

"Hello."

"Sharon, this is Nick. I have some bad news for you," I said before she had a chance to say anything.

There was dead silence on the other end.

"Sharon? Are you still there?"

"Yes," she replied with a heavy sigh.

"I'm sorry, Sharon, but Jeff was killed tonight," I said, not knowing what else to say.

Giving this kind of news was always difficult for me. I never knew what to say, or what kind of reaction I was going to get. In this case, I got nothing but silence.

"Sharon?"

"Yes?"

"Did you hear me?"

"Yes," she replied softly. "What happened?"

I took it slow and easy. I told her how he died and what was going on. I sort of left out the part about Miss Marshall. She cried for a while, then thanked me for calling her. I told her I would come by to see her as soon as I could get back to the Chicago area, then hung up.

I looked over at Monica and let out a sigh. It was over. We were done here except for maybe an interview with Sam in the morning to make sure that he had all the details correct. After that Monica and I could return to Madison with a brief stop at Sharon's to make sure she was doing okay.

"Nick, would you make love to me?" Monica asked as she looked at me.

A night like this one brought the realization that life could be short and that it could end at any moment without warning. I needed Monica as much as she needed me. I was not going to let one moment go by without taking the opportunity to show her how much I loved her.

I stood up and reached out to her. I took her hand and helped her up. As I put my arms around her narrow waist, she reached up and put her arms around my neck. We leaned toward each other until our lips met.

It was a warm, yet passionate kiss that expressed not only our love for each other, but also our desire for each other. I could feel her body pressed against me as I held her tightly in my arms. I could not resist the temptation to run my hands down her back and over her the smooth lines of her backside.

As our kiss ended, she looked up at me with those beautiful cobalt blue eyes. They sparkled with her love for me.

"I like having you hold me," she whispered in that soft sexy voice of hers.

"I like to hold you," I replied as I gently squeezed her bottom.

It didn't take long for us to get out of our clothes and climb into the king size bed. As soon as I laid down, Monica rolled up on top of me. The feel of her warm sexy body as I ran my hands up and down her back was all it took to clear my head of anything but her.

"Make love to me," she whispered.

How could I refuse such a request? I loved her more than life itself. She was everything to me.

I gently rolled her over on her back and looked down at her. The sparkle in her eyes and the feel of her sexy body were all it took for me to realize just what I had with her. I slid my hand up her side and over one of her firm breasts as I leaned down and covered her mouth with mine. We kissed passionately for several minutes before we lost ourselves in our love for each other.

www.ingramcontent.com/pod-product-compliance
Lightning Source LLC
Chambersburg PA
CBHW061137170626
46809CB00003B/895

* 9 7 8 0 9 9 1 6 2 3 2 7 3 *